Love and Happiness

Love and Happiness

Galt Niederhoffer

ST. MARTIN'S PRESS

NEW YORK

LOVE AND HAPPINESS. Copyright © 2013 by Galt Niederhoffer. All rights reserved. Printed in the United States of America. For information, address St. Martin's Press, 175 Fifth Avenue, New York, N.Y. 10010.

www.stmartins.com

Book design by Jonathan Bennett

Library of Congress Cataloging-in-Publication Data

Niederhoffer, Galt.
     Love and happiness / By Galt Niederhoffer.—First edition.
        p. cm.
     ISBN 978-0-312-64373-7 (hardcover)
     ISBN 978-1-250-03521-9 (e-book)
     1. Women motion picture producers and directors—Fiction.   I. Title.
  PS3614.I355L68 2013
  813'.6—dc23

                                                              2013002634

St. Martin's Press books may be purchased for educational, business, or promotional use. For information on bulk purchases, please contact Macmillan Corporate and Premium Sales Department at 1-800-221-7945, extension 5442, or write specialmarkets@macmillan.com.

First Edition: September 2013

10   9   8   7   6   5   4   3   2   1

For Erdun Gao

Acknowledgments

Thank you, Eebie (aka Elizabeth Beier). I admire and adore you. The wonder of your mind is matched only by your generosity, your patience, your hilarity, your turns of phrase, your vast knowledge, your friendship, your cooking, *and* by the pleasure of knowing you.

Thank you, Joy Harris, loving and beloved guide. I admire and adore you, too. I am grateful for your wisdom, your loyalty, and your example.

Thank you, Magnolia, Grover, and Elliot, for being you. Thank you, Dad, for telling me to. Thank you, Jonathan, for seeing things the way you do.

Love and Happiness

One

Sex with Sam had never been particularly good. He had always done his best to please and this was poignant, if not meaningful, to Jean. But as time began to dull Jean's sense of pleasure and acceptance, she faced the inescapable truth that this was to be the love in her life, that this was what she was to know of lust, of sex, of passion.

The morning's bout of romance had done little to solve the problem.

"Oh honey, you feel so good right now."

"Oh Sam." Jean upped the breathing.

"Oh honey, you're so beautiful."

"Oh honey, you're so handsome."

"Oh God," said Jean. A jabbing sensation spiked from her groin to her backbone.

Sam stopped and shifted his weight.

They stared at each other, eyes locked, bodies meshed,

Jean feeling, in the place where lust should live, its utter absence.

"You okay?" asked Sam.

"I'm fine," said Jean. She homed in on a crack in the ceiling. They stayed like this for several seconds, intertwined yet unconnected.

Taking silence as a sign, Sam renewed his efforts. They worked back into the whole giddy ruse with the best of intentions.

"Aah," said Jean.

"What is it?" asked Sam.

"I think I just ripped a muscle."

And with that, he tumbled off and acknowledged the greater rupture.

For Jean and Sam, marriage had caused a rip, a stark separation, a sailing away from the comforts of youth, among them sex, leisure, free time, unencumbered thoughts, all of which had been exchanged overnight for the hallmarks of married life, and then, five years and nine months later, for the infinite privilege and burden of shaping tiny humans.

They had settled into a comfortable routine, fulfilled plans, dotted i's, checked boxes.

"But nothing could prepare them for what happened that summer."

"Can we kill the movie taglines?" said Jean.

"Come on," said Sam. "They're funny."

"Not when you spend your days trying to solve exactly that problem."

"Jean, don't be so serious," said Sam.

Jean paused, choked back annoyance, did her best to smile despite the pain bisecting her body.

"Sometimes," said Sam, "forever has to get worse before it gets better."

Jean breathed out, nodded.

"Two grown-ups. Two children. One bathroom," said Sam. "Will they escape certain destruction?"

Jean had to smile at this. "Everyone loves the horror genre."

Sam stopped and stared at Jean, squaring off her brown eyes with his blue ones. "What would make you happy?" said Sam. "It's getting harder to decipher."

"Love, sex, help with the kids," said Jean.

"Sex with me?" asked Sam. "Or someone else?"

"With you," said Jean. And then to herself, *and maybe the occasional ex-boyfriend.*

Jean was not exaggerating. She had lost that loving feeling. She found the thought of two touching bodies mildly nauseating. Whenever she thought about sex, it seemed a desperate and inelegant endeavor. The words "dry hump" and "rub" came to mind. She pictured wild animals mating. She imagined her tits being tugged and poked like dough on a baker's table. She thought of unbecoming hair, rough skin, groping, clutching, panting, leg chafing leg like campers' twigs—God forbid a pair of lovers set a bed on fire.

She could not remember a time in her life when yearning had coursed through her, when her body had hungered for another body, been host to pleasure, sensation. And yet she felt no compulsion to recover the craving. It was as though her brain had been scoured and raided by a brilliant surgeon. With the curl of the knife, he had nixed the female brain's power center, excising desire itself from the cerebellum. Weirder still, Jean found this to be a plausible state of being. One did not long for longing, she discovered, once passion was fully absent.

Libido had little to do with it, nor did any of the typical reasons. Days earlier, Jean had declared the death of her sex drive with all the certainty of Alfred Kinsey. At the time, she was seated on a stationary bike next to Noelle, her friend and colleague. They were riding, according to their spin teacher, across the Serengeti, an improbable feat of imagination considering they were trapped in a dank black room with condensed sweat fogging the mirrors, tracing the very fine line between denial and self-awareness.

"Sex is overrated," Jean whispered.

"Oh Jean," said Noelle. "That makes me sad. Just to hear you say that."

"I guess there was a time when I would have found that statement tragic. But now that I've breastfed two babies, I'll never again find it. . . ." She stopped, sucked air.

"Find what?" Noelle asked.

"Find sex sexy."

"Please," said Noelle. "You just need a new—"

"Don't say vibrator."

"I wasn't going to say that. I was going to say new adventure. A new guy to picture."

Jean had come to accept just this as the bounds of her sexuality—her imagination—and its outline, the aging, rounding form that separated her and sex from their once intimate relationship. Common sense, of course, has never been imagination's deterrent. And yet, for Jean, sex had become a mystery so elusive, an exotic creature so hard to spot she had simply stopped staking it out, abandoned her tent for base camp: family, a fulfilling job, and a sexless marriage.

Many will argue that, for a girl, imagination trumps titillation; it's love that triggers lust, not lust that triggers all the excitement. Plunk a girl in a clean white lab in front of a slide projector and click away on the spotlit screen: a single red rose, a man in briefs, a skyline, a sunset. The subject should be on the floor sweating and heaving while her male counterpart comes to life at the first sight of undergarments. And yet, for Jean, even tried-and-true triggers failed her. Her imagination had gone limp. Her brain was dry and shriveled. She could not even imagine imagining sex. It was a distant galaxy in a fading black hole and Jean was a satellite spinning into someone else's orbit.

Jean feared she had decoded the truth about her sisters,

the fact that launched the thousand ships, the force that powers Facebook. Female sexuality, Jean decided, is not unlike a peacock. The very moment it sidles up, it's gone in a flurry of feathers. At times, it truly seems to crave warmth and admiration. At others, it turns away from love, allergic to human kindness. But most of all—and this is perhaps the only thing on which it can be counted—it seeks to defy whatever rules are ascribed to it, fueling desire with desire, desire that cannot be requited, until that desire flames out, like a spotlight in a blackout.

Jean turned now to face her pillow, breathed into the fabric while Sam clomped off without a word, acting very pious. The sound of his feet on the floor was followed by the patter of children's, their presence making the morning's misfire slightly less galling. Jean rolled over and batted at the drawer of her bedside table. The pink plastic case for her birth control was shiny as candy—as were the twenty-eight unopened pills routinely eschewed in favor of the rhythm method. It's not that she wanted more children with any active awareness; it's that the sex was infrequent enough that the chance was nonexistent. And perhaps the theoretical risk imbued conjugal sex with a much-needed element of excitement.

They heard the children at the same time, but Sam gave the better performance. He stood in the bathroom, brushing his teeth, gazing at his reflection in the mirror as though peering in would bring him closer to self-knowledge. He kept up the act for seconds as the children's calls escalated. Jean paused at the bathroom door and delivered a meaningful glower, then, exhausted by the idea of the fight, advanced to her hollering children.

The Banks lived on two floors of a blameless Brooklyn brownstone, a homestead blessed seven years ago by Jean's rose-colored glasses. Thanks to these, the peeling structure had appeared as a towering mansion, a project they could one day call a home—provided their incomes tripled and Sam developed a knack for home improvement. But as the economy scribbled on their tidy blueprints, the apartment graduated from a project to a problem, from something with "amazing potential" to an overwhelming nuisance, a progression, Jean often noted, that was not unlike their marriage.

The house was tainted by one major defect of construction, a relic of Victorian structures built throughout Brooklyn. A central staircase extended from the ground floor to the roof, an ovular spiral and, within it, a hole into which you could gaze from any floor and drop laundry or a penny or, if you leaned far enough, fall to your death in an elegant swan dive.

"I'm obligated to tell you," the real estate broker had told Jean and Sam on their second viewing, "these banisters are not up to code and need a little refreshment." And then, with a patronizing pat, "I'd look into this sooner than later, given that you're expecting."

A very pregnant Jean teetered precariously behind her. "Expecting what?" she'd wanted to say. "Certain death or certain children?"

"I find, with children, as with men," the broker went on to say, "they'll basically ignore it if you don't draw too much attention. It's when you say it's forbidden that you have a problem." She winked at Sam as if to say she could keep any secret. And the couple, though perfectly horrified, made fun of the broker all the way home, then promptly submitted their offer.

The stair remained an open debate up to the current moment, causing Jean to shudder every time the children went silent. They made various attempts to engineer a version of prevention, winding a net around the stairs from the ground floor to the skylight, extending the banister with plywood, and installing a Lucite extension. The rigs only made the staircase look strangely more decrepit and colluded with the general sense that just beneath the surface of family life lay clear and present danger.

The muddle of the television crept into Jean's thinking, a feature on a strange structure in New York's outer boroughs. The monument of sorts was built for the World's Fair in 1967, a sixty-foot ornate globe, a steel maze of oceans and continents that straddled the BQE between Queens and Long Island. The structure was a testament to midcentury excitement. It was dubbed the Unisphere and, though planned for a two-year stint, had been left to weather forty years of global warming and heavy traffic. On the show, a buff female engineer traversed the globe in a harness, finding the spots with the worst decay, homing in on the hot spots. She answered the newsman's questions as she dangled between Cuba and the Caribbean islands.

"It's a study in progressive decay," she explained. Jean decided not to share the phrase with her husband.

Somehow, Sam and Jean had sustained many years of rational pessimism, focusing on the positive even as their incomes stalled and their cost of living doubled. Holding on would surely prove the wise decision in the long run. Holding on was the new American Dream—it's what everyone was doing. It was as though the entire generation had bought IKEA's starter kitchen only to find, midassembly, they'd been following the wrong instructions. But the general state of the world acted as both foil and accomplice. If they were going down, Jean felt, then at least they could go down with the solace that others were going down with them.

From an aesthetic perspective, the place was the picture of charming. A stoop instead of a picket fence; red brick instead of white clapboard; strollers, idling ice cream truck, muffled screams from nearby playgrounds. Every morning, the street was scrubbed by the city's robust sunrise. Every night, lamplight transformed the building into a Halloween pumpkin.

The apartment was decorated in the typical fashion of parents, with a tacit decision to favor safety over anything more attractive. A stately leather sofa peeled as though it had once been painted. Magic Marker added polka dots to fabric hauled back from Thailand. Rugs and chairs, tables and desks, the yield of careful flea market culling, skirted the line between cozy and messy. The apartment was a monument to Jean and Sam's wise choices, proof that a life can be made like cake, provided with the right ingredients and correct timing.

Two

It started innocently enough. Jean liked the color of Sam's T-shirt. She was twenty-five. He was twenty-six, nursing big artistic dreams by night; by day, icing cupcakes. Jean saw him through the window as she waited in line for baked goods. His eyes were the same color as the sky, a shade of blue so promising it could only ensure disaster.

"I'm Jean," she said.

"I'm Sam," he said.

"What's your favorite flavor?"

"I like the devil's food cake," he said, "but I'm not an expert."

"Why so hard on yourself?" asked Jean.

He smiled. "I just moved here."

"Where from?" she asked.

"Ohio," he said.

Jean squinted, digested.

"And you?"

"Lived here all my life. Born and raised in Brooklyn."

"Wow," he said. It was the first time Jean had heard the word uttered in earnest. She studied the cake under a glass dome as though it were in a test tube.

Sam lifted the glass as she stared and presented a slice dripping with frosting.

Jean accepted with delight, took a bite with gusto, certain she had met her new best friend—and possibly the love of her life.

Jean looked back as she left the store to commit the exchange to memory. Sam sat at the icing station, framed by the window. Outside, the city was gray and pink, all innocence and potential.

Jean was still licking frosting off her hand when she called Information.

"Hi, it's Jean," she said when he picked up.

"I'm sorry," said Sam. "Who is this?"

"You forgot me already?"

"I know who this is. I just can't believe you're calling."

Jean smiled, affirmed by the praise. "You want to meet up later?"

A pause and then a thwacking sound as the phone hit the counter. "Sorry," he said. "Is midnight too late?"

"I'll meet you on the corner."

It should have been clear to Jean at this point that Sam

was a bit on the meek side, but Jean was a bit on the impulsive side and wrote it off as a cultural difference.

She sat down on a stoop near the bakery and remained
there for the next three hours, but for five minutes at the corner deli, where she bought provisions: a pack of cigarettes, a
new lip gloss, and a thingy of mascara, props she only used
when attempting a major performance.

Sam ambled toward the stoop just after midnight. Jean
fumbled with the cigarette she had been saving for the big
entrance.

"You smoke?" Sam asked.

"Sometimes," Jean said. She puffed with attention to
detail.

"You sure about that?"

"No. I guess not."

"Good," he said. "Me neither."

They proceeded to a nearby bar and situated themselves
at the jukebox, pooled enough quarters to do the laundry
of an entire building. Within an hour, both were drunk
enough to begin the confession process, compiling the list
of life's top ten—movies, books, music—on which young
lovers collaborate at the start of a relationship, as though
they must agree on ground rules before going any further,
as though common affinity predicts anything more than one
good conversation.

They enlisted a notebook from Sam's bag to commemorate

the archive. A few pages of scribbles fell out, revealing Sam's secret passion.

"You write?" Jean asked.

"I draw," he said. He fumbled with the notebook, sheepishly turning the page to reveal an illuminated manuscript, pages of ballpoint diagrams as detailed as a shipman's journal. Each panel was a moment of time, an instant, perfected.

"What are those?" Jean asked.

"They're storyboards."

"You want to be a cartoonist?"

"No," he said. His eyes were wide.

"I want to be a director."

"Wow," said Jean. It was the first time in her life she had uttered the phrase in earnest.

"You like them?" he asked.

Jean nodded and smiled. "No," she said. "I love them."

Which made him blush, etched the moment in time, and laid claim to Sam's heart at the very moment when it was most vulnerable to capture.

One by one, Sam's characters took residence in their collective consciousness. Weeknights were spent writing the script, weekends making the movie. Puppets, pom-poms, papier-mâché—anything was game for their early experiments. Together, they began to amass a body of work, an oeuvre. Jean would position while Sam would click. Sam would shoot while Jean would pose. Countless terrible and terribly sweet films went into production.

The Adventures of Sunset and Jane was a raucous tale in the style of a Tarantino road trip; two sock puppets sneak out of their drawer and light out for freedom, leaving a wake of hostages and blazing a trail of glory.

Lonesome Sam, a Bildungsroman about Sam's suburban childhood, in which names of friends and family were changed—to protect the innocent and the boring.

The Last Man on Earth, a twist on the dysfunctional family comedy, a searing portrait of the American household, also an apocalypse movie and, best of all, the perfect low-budget film because it required only one actor and only hilltops for locations.

Just like this, an archive emerged of two young idealists.

"We're so lucky," Sam had told Jean. They were perched awkwardly on a Brooklyn street with a view of the East River, timing their work to hit at the intervals between traffic. From this slope somewhere near the Gowanus, the city glowed pink and orange.

"Why is that?" Jean looked up to check for approaching vehicles and, finding none, hurried to move the arm of their puppet.

"Most relationships fail," said Sam.

"That's a sad statistic."

"Ours won't," Sam said. He didn't move. He looked at Jean through the camera.

"Why not?" said Jean.

"Because we're building something bigger."

Jean stood up from the ground and looked at her young husband. Perhaps he was right. She was playing with puppets on the street. Theirs must be a love with enduring power.

For the next few years, these same ingredients—youth and hope in heaping spoonfuls—yielded a sweet and hearty romance. And for the next few, it sustained their needs like a balanced, wholesome breakfast. And now they were here, ten years later, in a classic domestic standoff. The ability for love to turn like milk and never regain its freshness—it fascinated Jean to no end, and begged the obvious question: could it ever be turned back? Or did it become something wholly different, something edible but acrid, like yogurt? The future of their marriage rested on this simple question. Perhaps Sam was right: forever had to get worse before it got better.

Three

That Jean could be a force on the phone was something of a surprise given that she faced a phone's greatest challenge. She was terribly shy. She was not a natural talker nor particularly gifted socially. If given the choice, she would rather sit in silence than speak. Still, she took on the task every day with admirable bravery, transforming with a click into the woman she wished she could be. She knew, of course, that no piece of plastic could change her fundamentally, that she was, at all times, the same person, the same irreducible thing. But like all good salesmen, she was sometimes capable of magical feats. Somewhere between hello and goodbye, that was the best of Jean.

She had spent the morning running through a list of random leads, her desk stacked with helpful tools—a warm cup of coffee, a clean legal pad, peppermint candies. Her office, though sparsely decorated, did its part to cheer her on: photos of friends, arms laced around Jean, in parkas and bikinis, proof of love, happy times, accrued memories. Movie posters hung on all sides, like deer busts tacked to the wall, each one a testament to the power of hope, the power of wishful thinking. But now it was nearing noon and Jean had little to show for the morning. She sat for a moment, breathing slowly, like a stranded sea creature. Then she looked at her list and into her heart and picked up the phone again.

The feel of the thing in her hand; the dial tone's monastic fifth; the press of each digit on her fingertips, a reminder: you exist. And then, the ring, a rosary, a promise, and a pitch: "loss, life is full of loss, but you, Jean, you can win."

"Hi, this is Jeanie Banks," she said. "I'm calling for Daniel Lang."

"I'm sorry. Your name again?" Followed by the usual insult: a confused pause, a beleaguered sigh, and a request for spelling.

A minute passed as Daniel was called. Jean sat in silent prep. Then, the rustle of silk, the clearing of throats, and Jean rose to attention.

"What can I do for you?" Daniel asked.

It was an awkward in. How could she promise the world to someone who felt that the favor was his? "What can I do for *you*?" said Jean. Always let him speak first.

"Did I call you?" Daniel asked.

"No," said Jean. "I called you."

A lesser woman might have slunk away right then and there. But not Jean. The sale began when the customer closed the door.

"I wanted to talk to you first," Jean began, "since we share a passion for these."

A moment passed, the moment in which an interested party would speak.

"It's a timeless tale of hopes and plans. A classic heroine's quest. A girl in a car on the open road but she's really fleeing herself."

"Hmm," said Daniel. "Tell me more."

Jean opened her mouth to speak, but paused as she heard a familiar sound, fingernails on plastic.

"We open on a married couple in the private realm. They're making love, doing their best, but it's clear that they can't connect. The wife gets up, drops the kids at school, heads to work, punches the clock. And instead of going home that night, she sets off on a quest."

"Didn't they make this last year?" he asked.

"No," said Jean. "*They* did not." And then, at a lower volume, "It's possible I pitched you before."

"Yes, that must be it." Something dropped—a paperweight or a rock. "So, how can I help," Daniel asked. Again, the click of a keyboard.

"We're set to start shooting in a week. Totally prepped and crewed up. I've raised the entire budget." A breath. "Except for the last little chunk."

"Who's in it?" he said.

Jean recited the list. Tim Rule, Jennifer Bates.

"And they're firmly attached?"

"Yup."

"How much?"

But here, she paused and—in that pause—the tide of interest lapsed.

Now Daniel took a moment to distinguish flourish from fact.

Jean stayed mum. The sale began when the customer pictured the act.

Jean took this time to reaffirm those things she knew to be true. She knew that Daniel had the ability to say "maybe," though not the power to say "yes." She knew that Daniel wore silk ties, shopped exclusively in the West Village. She knew that Daniel had a lovely wife, a model or an editrix. And she knew that Daniel had stopped listening, that Daniel was about to pass and, once Jean knew these things about Daniel, she too lost interest.

"Here's the thing," Daniel said finally. "Everything about it is great. I love the dreary, gritty world, the sharp sardonic tone. I like the odd, haphazard route, how it favors voice over plot. I like the girl's ruthless willingness to hang on her own rope. I like that she's unlikeable and that's saying a lot." Daniel too, it must be said, had an innate sense of his power. He knew that rejection was best received with a delay and a dangling promise.

But Jean was already on to the next. She knew the pass as well as the pitch. She was already on to the next name, scrolling down her list. Time had honed these strategies and now it was innate. This was how she found hope in the face of disappointment: because her use for the customer ended as soon as he used her up.

"Given the state of the market," Daniel said, "we're just looking at genre right now. Action, horror, torture. Things you can watch without speaking English."

"Totally understand," said Jean. "That makes perfect sense. I'll try back in a couple of weeks to see if things have picked up."

With that, Jean replaced the phone in its cradle and sat in silent thought, comforted, though not consoled—never consoled—by the fact that she had hung up first.

To an outside observer, it might have appeared Jean had entered a meditative state. She replayed the most recent call in her head, every word and every misstep, reviewing her most effective moves and her biggest mistakes. It worked as a medicinal balm on her disappointment, soothing the bumps before they could bruise, the scrapes before they could scar, and cataloging various plays for future reference.

Like an athlete, she remembered every footstep, every point and foul, archived them all in a corner of her brain like plays on a chalkboard. It was sometimes painful to relive so soon after the fact. But she took solace in this: no matter how galling the loss, how crushing the disappointment, rejection like this would have been ten times worse in person.

Jean-on-the-phone was, of course, no different from Jean-in-the-flesh. And yet, the first one had an edge: she wore a mask. A pretty mouth, light pink and heart-shaped, charmed when turned up or down. Her thick brown hair could look, in turns, bookish or mysterious. Eyebrows furrowed endearingly when she had deep thoughts. All in all, her looks conspired with her accomplishments. Her greatest weakness was the one she wore right on her sleeve: her emotions owned her every move—a handicap in a job in which crushing highs and lows were an everyday occurrence. One hundred "no's" for every "yes." It was a world that ran on rejection.

So why did she put herself through these trials, this routine discouragement? Because the triumphs, however fleeting, were intense enough to addict. Making a sale was better than sex, better than any street fix. It was proof, more certain than any pinch, that you had had an effect, that you were here and here was real and perhaps, if heads were put together, something big could happen.

Any salesman will attest to the power of that moment. You have made a person act. You have caused a transaction. Your customer, simply by saying yes, has joined you in a sacred pact in which two strangers meet and affirm the other's existence. The dependence of the salesman on his customer and the customer on the sale takes effect. Everything, changes. Power transfers. And all it takes is a "yes."

The trick, Jean had learned, was to keep this in mind in the interim: that those who appeared to sanctify her, in fact, depended on her for purpose.

And to block out the last pitch the moment it ended.

A quick assessment of her desk reminded her of her progress. Pads stacked, candies wrapped, pens loaded for notation. The bauble-headed thingy on her desk still quivered with excitement. The murky blue rug on the floor remained unvacuumed, creating the sense that Jean was lost at sea, that her desk was her bobbing lifeboat. How did she sustain hope in the face of this daunting vista? She cleared her throat and forced a smile. Seven little numbers were all that stood between her and self-realization.

Now again, she picked up the phone, pressed her fingers to the keypads. And then, the ring, the sweet and obsolete sound of salvation.

"Hi, this is Jeanie Banks," she began.

"How can I help?" said the receptionist.

Jean paused. How to respond? "*Can* you help?" she wanted to ask. And more to the point, would you? If I were on a ledge, would you talk me down? Would you even stick around?

"Hello," said the receptionist. "Is anyone there?"

The question compounded Jean's confusion. Was she anyone today? Would she be tomorrow? Was anyone somebody always? Was somebody anyone ever?

The wondering quickly worked its way from idle thoughts

to full-blown panic. She thrust the phone back into its bank and stared at it, pulse throbbing, as though the device itself was the source of opposition.

A minute passed as she sat, collecting herself. When her pulse receded somewhat, she forced herself to try another.

Jean's cold call lists were given as a gift from Noelle. Noelle did the same thing as Jean—only six feet away in the next office. If seen from outside, in profile, back-to-back, stationed at their sooty windows, they might have seemed to be person and shadow, a model of fluorescent New York travail, a cartoon of repetition.

"These will come in handy one day," Noelle told Jean when she bequeathed the lists.

"Thanks," said Jean. "Very much." She stared at the smudged list in her hands, then looked to Noelle, who stood at the door, head craned like a flamingo.

"Drink a cup of coffee before you start."

"Will do." Jean nodded.

And then, as Noelle closed the door, "Or a cup of cyanide."

The cold call list served as something of a morning warm-up, like scales for an opera singer, only in Jean's case, the exercises served somehow to lessen the hopes of the performer. And yet, neither Jean nor Noelle dared overlook a potential customer. They knew that the most fruitful pitches could be found in the most unpredictable places, like gold from a river, and so forced themselves to pick up the phone even when their voices were hoarse.

Jean had spared no efforts in her search for investors. She found them in all sorts of ways—by referral, by cold call, by introduction. Once, she went as far as to take out an ad in a respected New York paper: EXPERIENCED INDIE PRODUCER SEEKS FINANCIAL PARTNERS. She got seventy calls the next afternoon. Certainly worth the price of the advertisement.

But Jean had learned most of all from her flubs and failures. The most important lesson was this: interest is not intention. The thrill of investing did not require completing a transaction. It began when he first sat down to meet, grew as he calculated margins. It heated up as Jean set the scene—scantily clad actresses, ski lodge negotiations—and continued as long as they kept up the ruse, if only in their imaginations.

The ratios were the same in every realm: pitching investors, actors, agents. Nine out of ten did not pan out, even after expressing interest—but that didn't stop them from talking. Talking was half the excitement. Over the years, Jean had compiled a glossary of sorts, a taxonomy of investors designed to aid early detection.

The Faker: at best a wishful thinker, at worst, a liar with a problem. He enjoyed the fun of the pursuit, got a charge out of playing a player, and compulsively pursued situations in which he upheld this falsehood. The Faker would gamble endlessly with money that was not in his possession, promising checks that never arrived, requesting dinner meetings. A Faker could go on for months with this odd performance, and so it was essential to identify him quickly or else waste time and risk financial ruin.

The Gambler: a version of the Faker. His fortune, though modest, did exist, but he had no intention of parting with it. He was prone to higher bids than the Faker, compelled to win at any cost, and pushed to greater heights with every new raise of the ante. The Gambler could sometimes be urged to act through traditional sales methods: a deadline, an ultimatum. But he usually got in over his head, forcing his spending capacity to more modest numbers. The Gambler, like the Faker, could be pushed to almost any height so long as he occasionally received the addict's kiss: a hit of nicotine, a charge of arousal.

The Skeptic: the polar opposite of the Gambler, a person whose inherent fear of loss eclipsed his appetite for risk. He was a cautious, innately scared person, a person who avoided conflict, a person who watched the weather report, carried an umbrella. Though the Skeptic could occasionally be enticed to sign a check, he required extensive persuasion. He used the term "due diligence" a lot, a process during which he listed the movie's flaws while exhausting his own pessimism.

The Loser: in theory a sitting duck but, in practice, a challenging target. One needed only play on his self-doubt to loosen his grip on his wallet. The Loser wanted most of all to renounce his days as a chubby adolescent, and to be admitted to parties from which he had been excluded. He was rich enough to come through in a pinch, but too shrewd to let go of his holdings.

The Dreamer: easy to intrigue, though trickiest to close, a customer who shared the salesman's romance, the ability to fall in love with a notion. The Dreamer was emotional by nature and so could be swayed with a pitch. But he was perhaps the most time-intensive because, in order to act, his dream had to match up perfectly with his salesman's. For two people's dreams to match up is a very rare occurrence. When it does happen, it's usually love, the most miraculous of all transactions.

In truth, there was only one sure thing, one reliable investor. This one had his heart in the game, a dangerous appendage, as it tended to made sudden movements and always beat out the cerebellum. This one wanted something specific, a standard trade for his money: a job for his son, a role for his girlfriend. He walked on the lot of his own accord, and this, Jean had realized over the years, was the best thing about him.

And yet, despite their differences, all investors shared one simple trait: they were less interested in the investment than the interaction. At the bone of all these conversations was not a calculation of profits, but rather a simple exchange in which two people tugged at either end of a rope, singing the duet of persuasion, doing the graceless dance of seduction, except without its clumsy climax. One person said "yes" while the other said "no"; one person said "pass" while the other said "fail"—and this silly stressful courtship culminated with a sale.

Jean finally left the office just before ten o'clock. She ducked into the subway on Thirty-fourth, caught the R to Central Park, sprinted from the platform up Madison, then ditched her sneakers and pulled on shoes that gave her more of an advantage. Their meeting spot was standard fare for an up-town investor: still-standing hedge fund wives and dowagers by day; by night, an assortment of disguised millionaires and boisterous Europeans. She located the correct person as soon as she entered. Bald head. Shiny face. Bright-eyed assistant, i.e., indentured girlfriend.

Jean made a series of calculations as she approached the table. The balding man in a decent suit was her prospective investor. The girl on his right was either a rebellious daughter or a very well-funded intern. She was introduced as his assistant, but her blush gave her away. They were sitting too close to be colleagues. And she looked too guilty.

"I won't waste any time," Don began. "I like your script a lot."

Jean allowed a nod. But she knew better than to smile so early in the meeting.

"I'm new to all this," he went on. "So I'll need a bit of guidance."

Jean looked at Don for a moment, tried to tune to his vibration. Don was hers, she decided. All she had to do was stay quiet.

"I won't bother pitching the script," she began, "since you've already read it. I'll just say, of all the deals on the market, this is the best investment." She took a deep breath, checked Don's eyes for the spark of attention. She found reserves in effort itself, like an electric car that charges while driving.

Don watched with a mellow smile, the exact expression Jean wanted. His lips curled up toward his nose, not to form a full-on smile, more of a line with curly edges. It was an expression she had seen before, an expression she worked for, the expression people made when they wanted to be sold—not unlike the expression people wear when they are watching a movie.

"The budget is tiny, the cast is huge, the script is very commercial. Tim Rule and Jenny Bates will star. We start shooting a week from tomorrow."

Don continued to stare at Jean with the same expression. People got this look, Jean had found, when they liked what they were hearing, when they saw that they were liked, and right after an orgasm. It was the look of a wish being fulfilled, the brain on serotonin.

"No need to go on," Don interrupted. "We're both busy people. I like what you're doing a lot. I'll tell you right now that I want it."

Jean nodded once again but refused any relaxation. "Glad to hear it," she said. "Do you have any questions?"

"I've made a lot of money," Don said, "in many different arenas, and I know enough to know when I don't know what I'm doing."

Jean opened her mouth to make a token disavowal. But she stopped herself just in time. Don was talking himself into the deal. The worst thing to do was interrupt. It was time to end the meeting.

"What I would like to do," said Don, "is learn the nuts and bolts. Work with someone who knows more than me, to become that person's shadow."

Again, Jean fought an impulse to relieve inner tension. He was doing the selling. *He* was doing the talking. Jean just had to stay out of the way, let him build momentum.

"Sure," she said. She found the word to be an all-purpose solution. "I'll call you in a couple of days to discuss the deal points."

Don smiled and paused as though waiting for further direction. His assistant offered her own hearty smile. They both made moves to stand, fumbled for their belongings. But Don delayed. He had something to say, but was having trouble saying it.

"You ever have a puppy?" he asked.

"Uh, yes," Jean said. "When I was little."

"They're awfully cute."

"Yes, they are. But now I have children."

"Children love puppies," Don said. "Maybe you should get one."

"Hmm," said Jean. "I'll think about it. My hands are full at the moment."

Don was clearly put off by this, but he quickly recovered. "I'm flying to LA in the morning."

"Oh," said Jean. "Sounds exciting."

"You're welcome to hitch a ride. On my plane. I imagine you have lots to do on the other coastline."

"Thanks," said Jean. "I'll keep that in mind. Right now, I have no cause to be there."

"You know what they say about private planes."

"No," said Jean. "Not familiar."

"You'll never go back again," said Don.

Back where? Jean wanted to ask, but she was already out and running.

Four

Jean returned to the office at an urgent clip, with the same manic enthusiasm she felt in the morning when the promise of the future was still untainted by the memory of past failures. Sitting down, she turned again to the list of her morning misfires. She stared at the phone, her steadfast companion, her loyal sidekick. The crackle of the connection. The harmony of potential. But suddenly her door was open.

"Jean?" said a voice. A token knock and then he was beside her.

"I stopped by to bring you coffee," said Sam. "And to give you a pep talk."

"Sam," said Jean. "How was the scout?" She adjusted her tone to sunny.

"I think we found a place in Jersey that will play for the Nevada desert."

Sam went on to explain the morning's triumphs. Jean did

her best to listen as an objective party, not as a wife watching her husband stare down his shaky future. How could she tell Sam at this moment, on the eve of his fruition, that the likelihood of its happening was currently one in a million?

"I'm not gonna lie. Morale was low when we crossed the GWB. It's gonna be a little like shooting sunlight on the aurora borealis."

Jean felt the muscles in her face begin to soften. This man, this dreamer, this hopeful fool was the reason for all of this trouble.

"But then I got this great idea and everyone got excited. Jersey is just like the desert," said Sam. "If you frame out the oil tankards."

The last ten years had not been especially kind to Jean's husband. His career had started strong at the gate with an early triumph, followed by a handful of minor films, each with diminishing prestige and lessening budgets. By thirty, he had nearly given up on the life of a young man artist. The last few years had seen a string of near-misses and disappointments with projects invariably falling apart at the last minute. Still, Sam was tireless, if not in his optimism, then in his commitment. Like most great artists, he was obsessed—and this made him both a handful and heroic.

Sometimes, Jean confused Sam's ambition with his love for her. They looked the same: the desire of a director trying to launch his project, and the desire of a man trying to get a woman's approval. She knew how ill advised it was for them to work together, but watching him struggle all those years as she gradually prospered—it seemed cruel to let him flail, like letting a toddler tie his shoelaces when you were already late for dinner.

She had lived to rue the decision.

Since they began working together, their relationship had changed drastically. Jean was Sam's pusher, his hookup. She had what he needed: the keys to his dream, the map to his treasure, and, on its circuitous path, all sorts of encouraging bread crumbs.

As it turns out, there is some fallacy to the popularly held notion that lovers collude to fulfill one's dreams, that love is the great conspirator. On the contrary, Jean had found in Sam not an ally, but an opponent. Of course, their love and history tempered feelings of obligation. But the impact was undeniable. Compassion is most challenging, it turns out, when required by one's protector.

Sam closed the door and lowered his voice to a whisper. "How is it *really* going?"

Jean smiled, forced air into her lungs. "You promised you would stop saying that."

"I'm sorry," he said. He leaned closer. "How's it going? Really."

"Great." Jean sighed. "Getting close."

"Getting close or getting closer?"

"Sam," said Jean. "This doesn't help."

"Please don't sugarcoat it, Jean. Better to know sooner than later."

"Sam," Jean said, raising her voice. "I need you to keep it together." She gestured at her office door, cocked her head toward the murmur of people working beyond it.

"I'm sorry," said Sam. He walked toward the glass and pressed his face to the window. He gazed down at the blurry city, the smudged edge of the building, then he crouched to kneel on the floor and began to whisper a prayer into the carpet. As he muttered, he reached into his pocket and set forth an array of objects—a coin, a candy wrapper, a ticket stub. He was making an offering. To whom? The God of Independence.

Jean peered down at her husband.

"Tell me what I can do," he said. "I'm the boat, not the drowning swimmer."

Jean smiled, nodded.

Sam rolled over onto his back like a dying beetle. "If you could just tell me how this works 'cause I'm a bit uncertain."

Whatever calm was brewing in Jean was once again shattered. "So we have a script," Jean began.

"Right."

"And we're trying to make a movie."

Sam nodded studiously, as though he were hearing this for the first time, as though he had not made a study of the business since his fourteenth birthday.

"But it's not like writing a book. You can't do it at your

desk, just you and your computer. And it's not like drawing a picture. You need more than crayons and construction paper. You've chosen an art form that requires significant cash and resources. People, places, costumes, lights, camera, equipment."

Sam nodded.

"It's a paradox," Jean said. "We need money to get the actors."

"Right," Sam said.

"And we need actors to get the money."

"Yes."

"So we find ourselves in a bit of a jam, a challenge worthy of a magician."

Sam's eyes widened. "Or a great salesman!"

"It's an art more than a science," Jean said. "A game more than a business."

"We need the actors to get the money," Sam said. "We need the money to get the actors." He was chanting and this was his mantra.

"Which leaves us between a rock and a hard place," said Jean.

"In other words, totally fucked."

"I prefer to look at it this way: totally prepped and crewed up."

Sam turned to face the radiator, took in the view underneath, a whole new array of objects.

Sensing that Sam was losing his grasp, Jean took a decisive

breath, stood from her chair, knelt down to the floor, and curled up beside him. They lay like this in total silence, two bodies, shoulder to shoulder, until Jean began to swoon under the heat of the radiator.

"I'm sorry," Sam said.

"It's okay," Jean said. "I know how badly you want this. But I need you to make me a promise."

"I promise," said Sam. "I promise."

Jean sighed, and on the exhale, decreased the space between them to zero. It was the closest she had felt to her husband in as long as she could remember.

"You can lie here for five more minutes," said Jean. "And then, you're going to go back out there. You're going to tell your crew they're here today because they're doing something important. They're going somewhere, Sam. And where are they going?"

"To find new jobs?"

"No," said Jean. "They're going where you tell them to go if you can tell them—tell us—where we are going, what it's going to look like, and how *we* are going to get there."

Sam looked at Jean from his supine position. It was a battle cry and Sam felt it. He smiled, kissed her on the lips, and jolted back into existence.

Jean loved this facet of negotiation, the way power transfers in an instant and, in that instant, reveals the locus of power in the first place. It was always and never there, just like the money and the actors.

The ringing phone offered Jean the interruption she needed. She pointed theatrically at her desk to signal that the call was urgent, causing Sam to spring to his feet and dutifully exit.

"Tim's having second thoughts." This was the caller's introduction.

"What do you mean?" said Jean. "You said he was fully committed."

"He mentally was for quite a while, but now he's not as certain."

"But Sam took all of his notes," said Jean. "They had great conversations."

"You know how fickle actors are. He's driven by his emotions."

"We shoot in less than a month," Jean said, her lungs constricting, compressing. "I financed this movie around him. This will end it. This will kill it."

"I'm sorry," said the agent. "He's made up his mind. He doesn't change his decisions."

"But you said . . ." Jean trailed off. There was no point in reviewing. "You have to talk to him now," Jean said. "Jobs, careers are at stake here. Investors have made investments. Deals have been signed. Equipment purchased."

"I get the conflict of interest," said the agent, "given your relationship to the director."

Jean felt the insult as a blow, exactly as intended.

"There's nothing I can do. Tim is very decisive."

"But he can't," said Jean. She shook her head as though this could negate what she was hearing.

"Maybe it would help if you talk to him, you know, get yourself out here, show up on set and kiss the ring, pay an official visit."

Jean nodded in response, forgetting the agent couldn't see her. But she was nodding less at the request than she was at her own conviction, attempting with this instinctual act to bring something to fruition. She resolved to share nothing of this to Sam—his panic would help no one—and quickly excused herself from the call to throw up in the bathroom.

When she returned, it was dark outside, the city rushing toward evening. The phone rang as she twisted the doorknob. To answer or not to answer?

Five

Jean made a point of finding her keys before she reached her door in an effort to avoid spending extra time facing yet another obstacle. Despite the complaints of friends and guests, she did not permit shoes in her home. It was a holdover from when her children were small, at first a hygienic measure, now a means of keeping the grime of the world out of her private sector. She removed her shoes at the door and grazed the floor in stockings. The feeling was not soothing in itself, but a harbinger of comfort to come, the first in a series of sensations that promised closure and quiet.

A crash and the sound of breaking glass greeted her as she entered.

Marty stood at the door, wearing a floral bikini. Jane stood a step behind, trying to reclaim her belongings. Jane deployed a combination of intimidation and force, one hand tugging at the bandeau, the other prying the underwear off as though she were peeling the rind from an orange.

Jean tried to take a step, but the door was blocked. Jane stood in the narrow passage, smiling at her triumph. With hair the color of carrot cake and eyes the color of denim, Jane already had an edge on her exhausted mother.

"Marty is chasing me," said Jane, "and he won't stop talking."

Jean put down her bag and settled in for a relaxing evening.

Marty's speech pathologist had inadvertently decoded the male gender with his first lesson in upper palate consonants. Marty and family were to engage in this simple role play.

"Rar!" said Marty.

"Ahh!" said the other person.

"Rar!" Marty was to say again.

"Ah!"

And so on, ad infinitum with Marty playing the enraged monster and the other playing his dismayed damsel. With this simple duet, the speech teacher offered an inadvertent insight, decoding the first challenge of human speech and the genesis of male-female behavior. The act of scaring and being scared, of chasing and running—this seemed to Jean to be at the heart of all male-female dyads. The extent to which this dialogue was a naturally occuring behavior or a consensual role play—this was less clear to Jean. For the moment, it functioned as neither, as Jane had tired of the game and Marty had devolved into a puddle of tearful whining.

"I know what I want for Christmas," Jane said, commandeering her mother's attention. Jane was a salesman like her mother, but a far more skilled negotiator.

Jean took another step, but Jane scurried ahead, blocking her path again.

Jane produced a rumpled piece of paper and began reading. "Dear Santa. How are you feeling? Are the reindeer warming up? I hope you are not too cold up there and here's my list for Christmas. One, an American Girl doll. Two, a new parka. Three, a hat with a pom-pom. Four, magical powers. First choice: invisibility. Second choice: flying. Five: peppermints for my mother. My brother will send you his own list but he doesn't deserve too much because he hit me on the forehead."

Marty lunged at his sister before she had finished reading. Jean stood between the two and acted as a human partition.

The list was rife with spelling errors and written in the shape of a stocking, but this somehow served to strengthen its negotiating posture.

The problems of adulthood and childhood converged with this year's dilemma: uphold the lie of Santa and its many deceptions, or fess up to the espionage and come clean sooner rather than later? Stronger marriages than Jean and Sam's had folded under the pressure. The insistence with which a parent upheld the myths of childhood was in direct proportion to that parent's betrayal. And yet, without up-holding these myths, how could one protect innocence and wonder? No decent alternative had yet to be invented.

A parent had two choices: a) run around in a red suit pre-tending to be an obese pagan, or b) condemn one's child to live in a world devoid of magic. Splitting the difference was not a good choice. Lying was not an option—nor was skirt-ing questions about his address, or downplaying the guy's existence, as this just left a kid with a sense of her parent as a half-assed person. At times, it seemed a losing proposi-tion for child and parent. And so the question echoed this year louder than ever: how could a parent preserve inno-cence when the very fabric had been corrupted? Would that Jean could answer this regarding both her family and her marriage.

Patience won the day this night, as with most others. At nine o'clock, after an hour of heated negotiations, the chil-dren finally gave in and knocked themselves unconscious. Jean and Sam reconvened and exchanged their first full sentence.

"How are we going to swing that?" Sam said.

"What?"

"The Santa wish list."

"Our daughter has designed the perfect test. She wants a happy childhood for Christmas."

"I've got a plan for the powers," said Sam. "We'll give her

some sort of certificate. Then when she decides to cash it, we'll walk around and ignore her for a while, pretend we can't see her."

"That's every woman's nightmare," said Jean.

"It'll be fine," said Sam. "Don't sweat it. It's the doll I'm worried about. Those things are expensive."

"It's like she's designed an impossible trial. Here's your chance, Mom and Dad. Let's see if you're good parents."

Jean stared down the hall as Sam emphatically nodded, did her best to combat the swell of self-doubt that routinely assaults all parents.

They exchanged a nod where a kiss had once been and a sigh where thrill was prior, then began their retreat to their separate corners, Sam traipsing into the bedroom, and Jean tiptoeing away to her hallway office.

Quiet regained, Jean hurried past her sleeping children. She landed at a desk pushed up against a narrow hallway, the horizontal area serving somehow to widen her sense of the future. No matter that its sea was greenish white plaster and its sky a framed poster of the New York skyline. The space somehow felt like a cocoon and earned its place in Jean's heart as nook and command center.

Here, Jean commenced her favorite part of the day, her nightly vesper. She sat at her computer in blessed silence and squeezed intimacy from the Internet like water from a washcloth. She sat like this for hours without the possibility of interruption, content that her closest friend in the world was a screen that had replaced the telephone, the television, the encyclopedia, the dictionary, the library, the calculator, the map, the compass, the book, and her husband. The irony was not lost on her—its promise to connect her to the world while ensuring her isolation.

Hands warmed by peppermint tea, Jean took in the day's first pleasure. By her estimation, she spent more time at her computer than any other living person. Between making calls, reading scripts, writing notes, and sending and receiving emails, it was fair to say that Jean was a slave to communication.

Just like this, Jean settled into her nightly ritual, an elaborate process whereby she pretended to work but, in fact, distracted herself. Jean was a human treadmill, an impossible math problem; with every step she took closer to her goals, she pushed herself farther from them.

At ten o'clock, she had no fewer than thirteen screens open on her computer. The television was set to Jon Stewart, computer host to Facebook, a half-read script, a Google search on Don Quixote's sidekick, and her cell phone cradled in her lap, poised to catch other morsels of intrigue, like a teaspoon in a rainstorm.

If her seat at her desk was her confessional, here began her prayers. Doug Chase was the central tenet in Jean's religion.

The first time Doug and Jean dated, they were still children. Jean was a sophomore and Doug was a senior at Kenyon, a post that granted him the right to advise on a range of issues from the style of Jean's prose to the style of her underwear. They fell wildly in love in the traditional sense, which is to say a war of attrition, ten acts of passion, heartbreak, and betrayal that came close to destroying each other, and several people within a five-mile radius.

Jean had just moved into swank off-campus sophomore housing, living out the collegiate dream down to the bicycle and fedora. After class, she biked home through leafy streets, head whirling with inspiration. She spent afternoons in a haze of ideas, reading and writing papers. "A Home Run for Homer, Tricks and Tropes in the Quest Structure"— this would be her sophomore thesis. The topic afforded Jean the time and intrigue for a happy existence.

Doug was teaching critical writing to blinking freshman girls, a population that regarded him with wholly uncritical gazes. He was living in an attic apartment with more dormer windows than square footage, subsisting on stipends and Ramen noodles while writing about the classical hero. Both were at a stage in their lives when everything felt possible. No dream was too grandiose, no nightmare too macabre.

They met by the copy machine in the English department. Doug was preparing handouts for his students and Jean was checking her email—or at least, making a very good pretense of it.

"Are you Jean?"

She nodded. He was shorter than the boys she usually liked, but his confidence caused him to tower above her.

"We're not supposed to meet," he said, raising a brow in a pantomime of danger.

"That's ominous," she said.

"You dated my friend Joe."

"Well, we're just friends now."

Doug smiled, studied Jean.

"That's right," Jean said. "He said we should meet."

"Which means he hoped we wouldn't."

Jean nodded slowly as though they had just shared classified information.

"I'll have to show you the town," Doug said. "All three of the hot spots."

"That would be fun," she said, then less coolly, "I don't know anyone."

They continued like this, with near-misses at wit and a poor performance of disinterest, lit, every ten seconds, by the copier's roving searchlight.

They exchanged the necessary platitudes, alluded to the requisite connections, established, with the usual flicker of badges, their mutual aspirations. But soon enough, these clumsy semantics would come to seem beneath them as they discovered that their favored mode of communication was telepathic. Tiring of banal platitudes and thinly veiled flirtation, they made tentative plans to meet the next day, then retreated to their classrooms, limbs limp, hearts pounding.

They met the next afternoon at the appointed local hangout and, after a skirmish with grad students, managed to secure a corner table. Within seconds, they had fallen madly in love in the traditional sense, which is to say the nervy, narcotic version that turns every tune into a theme song, every passing thought into an email that needs to be written. But that afternoon, and for the next several months, they proceeded with caution.

First, they agreed on the greats—writers, poets, musicians—then they conspired on a list of life's most overrated, cut vast swaths through the Western canon as though they alone had been appointed to judge art and beauty. The date ended with a promise to trade work, the usual fumbling for the bill and one drink over the sensible limit. As they teetered out, Doug made the token offer for a ride—transportation as seduction. And within twenty minutes, they were making out in the front seat of his Volvo.

The relationship accelerated from there with impressive pickup. For a year, they enjoyed the perks of love—the attraction, the nausea, the elation. By the end of the year, they had reached the point at which love either reinvents itself or begins to go sour. Like mountain climbers scaling a peak, both grew somewhat delirious, finding their goals receding with every step in the right direction. At the height of it all, both were confronted with love's most damning quality: the way it demands ever higher dosages to re-create that first mind-blowing feeling.

By the end of year one, it was clear to both they would not end up together, a decision they confirmed—and consoled—with a long, protracted breakup. There were late-night appearances on doorsteps, proposals, tearful phone calls, jealous rages. But in the end, all these gestures came to seem like childish theatrics. Within a year, both Jean and Doug had found less emotional partners and begun the march toward marriage. Separately, they would curse the drama, feign relief at skirting disaster, and, in late-night hours, wonder if they had chosen the wrong person.

Now, nearly ten years later, Douglas Chase had resurfaced. He owned her heart, eclipsed her thoughts. She lived for him, and he knew it. Jean wrote to Doug once a day, a short, perfunctory update, sharing a snapshot of her life or a friendly query. She funneled much of her creative energy into these emails. She was at her best when she wrote to Doug, certainly at her freest, likely because she wrote these notes with the knowledge that no one would ever read them.

This cache of unsent emails accrued to form an impressive archive. It was not exactly a correspondence—still, a dialogue, if one-sided. The notes were steeped in emotion—grief, longing, ambition—confessionals kissed with the freedom of truth, the promise of the uncensored. The writing was, as a result, wholly unself-conscious, prose more honest than the kind shared with another living person.

Jean was not unaware that the cause of all this ardor

might not be Doug at all, but some sort of placebo. Time or memory had, for Jean, turned a kind of spigot, unleashing a rush of feeling like icicles in a heat wave. In a sense, Jean's mode of submission ensured that the letters remained kalei-doscopic, on one hand creating a cache to rival the letters between Elizabeth and Darcy, on the other, amassing a shipman's log of life's disappointments.

It was a study in the subjunctive. Jean would never know whether Doug would have responded, and if he had, what he would have written, what he would have omitted. Would he praise her mind, her looks as he had when they dated? Would he say he worshipped her, that he couldn't live without her? Would he cushion her sorrow with longing, her demands with compliance? Would he or would Jean win the most intense negotiation? The one between loved ones.

But Doug didn't couldn't—respond, which made the letters all the better. They lost the tension of suspense, the wondering, the waiting, the guesswork, even as they gained a new power, the sheer weight of their duration. And then, that most elusive force—the tide of a narrative: pacing, emotion, setup, payoff. Jean could write anything she liked and Doug would disappoint always and never. She was writ-ing a novel, one whose only audience was its writer.

Despite the freedom of the voice, the intrinsic logic of the structure, the letters carried the sting of a romance, and the swell of an epic. They constituted a mourning period, a vigil for something, a vigil for time, for memory, for a love that was dead and buried. The emails were, therefore, not so much about Doug as they were about longing, about the way we crave what is gone, sometimes even when—even more because—we have lost track of what is missing.

Jean was fully cognizant of the folly of the project. It was a variation on a theme, a riff on a familiar melody. Writing Doug was another version of what she did all day: trying, failing, trying again, buying and selling. Jean pitched herself to Doug. Only here, she was salesman and product.

At home, as in the office, she had one tool at her disposal: no voice, no face to hide behind; just the hope of moving a person with words. Simple enough. Like swaying a sky-scraper with a whisper.

On a lark, Jean fired up Facebook and scanned his recent broadcasts. She spent the next hour at her computer, craft-ing the perfect message.

"Doug," she wrote, "don't you miss us?"

Too naked. She paused, deleted.

"Doug, you good?"

Too oblique. He might think she was actually interested in how he was feeling.

"Doug, meet me for a drink. Rough day at the office."

Too cliched, too desperate.

"Doug, have some very big news. Meet me at Frankie's in an hour."

A good salesman didn't have needs. She simply presented an offer.

She pressed Send before she could question herself and stared at the screen, breathless.

The response arrived in ten seconds. "See you there."

Jean leaped from her desk, hurried down the hall, and attacked her closet.

Sam lay on their bed, eyes glazed and immobile. Jean rushed in with the hope that speed would prevent him from noticing her attire and the large sweater under which it was hidden. She blew him a kiss from the door and mumbled something unintelligible, explaining she had an emergency meeting with an investor.

"Hence the overly low-cut top and the excessive fragrance?"

"What?" said Jean. She paused at the door. "I'm trying to get your movie funded."

"You don't dress like that for me," Sam said.

"You don't have millions of dollars."

Jean laughed to bring home the joke, though Sam was not laughing. Then she rerouted down the hall and locked the front door behind her.

Ten minutes later, she was sprinting in heels through cobblestoned Brooklyn, her skirt hiking closer to her waist with every step forward. She hailed a cab and darted inside with all the grace of a pony, then gave the driver the address and attempted to apply mascara in the reflection of the cab's plastic partition.

Jean met Doug at a spot trendy enough to make her feel silly, a place with an abundance of kitten heels and guys in tight, elasticized jeans that made their legs look like insects.

"Hey," he said.

Jean regretted the decision within seconds. It was painfully clear she had come from home—and that she had dressed for the occasion.

"Jeannie, how've you been?" said Doug.

Jean stalled, debated. There were two approaches to human interaction: feign happiness or be honest. "Fabulous," she said.

"Really?" he asked.

Jean paused. What had she said that gave her away? "Why? Do I not look okay?" She had backed into the worst possible approach: begging for approval.

"No, I mean. Yes. You look great."

Jean smiled.

"Just different." And then: "You sure everything's okay? I thought I detected a note of sadness."

Jean paused, peeved by her clumsiness, impressed by his intuition. It would take a massive landslide now to regain footing.

"Sam and I are getting divorced," she announced.

"Aha," he said. "I knew I detected a darkness. Or was it excitement?"

Jean smiled, shifted her gaze, confused by her own declaration. She opened her mouth to clarify, then realized the question was better left unanswered.

Doug was, she confirmed, only getting more handsome. His skin had been buffed by the cold, causing his cheeks to look pink and shaven. His face had thinned out over the years, carving a ruddy athletic face with cheekbones and distinction. A curly mop of hair had once given him a rakish appearance. Now he looked somehow scholarly, an impressive feat for a man who never finished the books he opened. Jean removed her hands from her face where she had subconsciously placed them.

"Do I look old?" she demanded.

"What?"

She waited in silence. "Do I look old?" she repeated.

Doug shifted uncomfortably, looked down, away—the classic gestures of avoidance.

"Please," said Jean. "You can tell me."

"Jean, you're putting me on the spot with this question."

"Doug, we've been friends for twenty years. You've seen me all kinds of naked. I need you to be honest."

Doug checked her eyes to ensure that her plea could be trusted, then ignored his better judgment and answered in earnest. "A woman shows her age in two places."

"Which places?" Jean demanded.

"The skin and the hair."

Jean waited. Was this her verdict or her indictment?

"You're fine," he said.

"Fine?" she asked.

"Yeah." He smiled. "For the moment."

"What does that mean?" Jean snapped.

"Hey," he said. "Don't get defensive. You'll have no trouble on the open market."

Jean tuned out effectively for the meeting's last awkward chapter. Two drinks later, she had, at least, attained a measure of detachment, reaching the point where one's thoughts can be tracked around the brain like moons around a planet.

In the cab back home, she ransacked her bag, passing over her blush and lip gloss. She clawed frantically for her phone as it proved to be, once again, both her shackles and the means of her liberation.

"Don," she said when he picked up the phone. "Does the offer still stand for a ride?" It did.

Then she called Tim's agent. "I'm flying to LA in the morning. Please tell Mr. Rule I'd like to pay him a visit."

Six

Jean returned to her bedroom and found it as she'd left it. Sam had fallen asleep sitting up, the light of the television searching his face like a policeman's flashlight. The blankets were bunched up in odd places, as though he had spent some time sampling various positions.

It slayed Jean to see her husband like this, at once passive and captive. When had a vital, passionate young man become this aging, empty vessel? Horrified by the thought that age alone could work this magic, she sat down on the side of the bed and unzipped his pants, testing her ability to experience and elicit arousal.

"What?" Sam said, his eyes still closed.

Jean paused, then continued her seduction.

"Honey," he said, swatting her hand away, "It's okay, I'm really tired."

It had been an apology of sorts, recompense for the

morning's misfire. And it leveled the field, Jean decided. They were now officially even. She had done her best to satisfy and the effort had gone unnoticed.

Jean watched him fall asleep, felt the familiar stab of disconnection, then shook his arm with too much force, as though she were testing his nerve endings.

"Sam," she said. "Wake up."

Sam's nerve endings seemed to be broken.

"Sam," Jean said. "Wake up. I have to go to LA in the morning."

"Do you want me to come?"

Jean shifted her weight. "Neh," she said. "The kids and the crew need you here. I'll ask my mother to stay over."

"How long will you be gone?" Sam asked.

"One night. Maybe two."

Sam stared at Jean for a moment, as though posing a tacit question. "Okay, knock 'em dead," he said, then he reverted to corpse position.

Jean stood and crossed the room.

"Let me be your wing man," Sam called.

"Thanks, but I fly solo." She regretted it the moment she said it.

Her bags packed, Jean slid through the house, passed her hallway office, stopped at the door of her children's room and stood, listening to them breathe, taking in the sound of their survival   in, out, in, out, an embrace and then a rejection.

Seeing one's child fall asleep is a strangely intense experience, terror mixed with relief, anger with nostalgia. Those first few moments of sleep combine a wealth of emotions for parents—the admission that one's child is a consuming force, the ultimate burden, and that one's child is mortal, her days and life numbered.

Overwhelmed by their innocence—the armies of stuffed animals, the framed images of cheerful frolic, Jean crawled into bed with her son and made a circle around his body.

"Marty," she whispered.

He didn't move, but seemed to know she was present.

"Marty," she said. She cupped her hands around his stomach, which was both taut and pliant. "Do you know how much I love you?"

"How?" he whispered.

"More than everything," said Jean.

"Oh," he said. "More than Jane?"

"No, not more than Jane," Jean said. "Both of you more than everything together."

Marty paused and recalibrated, disappointed by the concession. "More than toys?" he whispered.

"Yes, more than toys." Jean pulled him closer so that his back was flush with her heart, his backbone aligned with her heartbeat. "Marty," she said.

"Yes," he whispered.

"I have to go on a trip in the morning."

"When will you be back?" asked Marty.

"Soon," she said. "Just two days. Will you save this spot for me?"

Marty paused. "Mommy," he said finally.

"Yes," said Jean.

"Will you bring me a present?"

Jean smiled. "Maybe, yes. If you go to sleep right this minute."

And she burrowed in close so that their bodies formed one waxing crescent.

Seven

Jean was not a fan of flying or, more specifically, of landing. No amount of fact or logic could influence her opinion. She understood Bernoulli's law, the basic physics of flying. She understood the statistics, the comparative risks of driving. She didn't mind the rush of wheels, the takeoff, the sudden lightness. She didn't mind the airport lines, the travelers' excitement. That is not to say that she enjoyed any of these aspects, but her chief concern during takeoff was more misanthropic: sharing the same air and germs with so many strangers.

What Jean feared was the descent, the straight shot to the pavement. In her mind, this was not an irrational fear, but rather a well-informed one based on a calculation of the speed and mass of falling objects. And the convulsion her body would make when the jet hit the pavement, exploding like a grenade—arms, legs, hands flying. The fear translated, during flights, into something like an explosion that burst from her throat to her chest down her arms whenever her heart won the fight with her mind, between common sense and better judgment.

Her fear of flying was so bad that, for many years, she had taken the train from New York to Los Angeles, which she was bound to do several times a year by reason of her employment. The low hum of the train was a more soothing companion, as were the sorry passengers and college kids heading home or to some better version. The train gave Jean a sense of calm, as though she were among family, or better yet, a crowded place full of kindred spirits.

It was the same feeling she got at night as a young insomniac when she turned on the radio to listen to people talking. Hearing people pose and answer even the most trivial questions provided a certain comfort, as though she was not alone in the dark, waiting for time to continue.

To Jean, arriving in LA by train was more honest than arriving by airplane. LAX, with its midcentury curves and magical palm tree procession, foretold an LA Jean did not love, an LA made of plastic. Jean much preferred the scale and weight of Union Station, its massive turn-of-the century bricks, the earnest, bloated arches, the out-of-place art deco leaves blossoming from sturdy pillars and, when you emerged from the train, clothes wreaking and hair matted, the stink of warm Chinese food, of sunlight and urine. Union Station was LA as it really was, a dried-out tropical oasis, an honest-to-goodness shithole.

But Jean had now spent several years conquering her fear of flying, developing the same relationship—love and hate—with the city at the end of the journey. Her choice of hotel followed the same circuitous logic: when she traveled to LA for work, Jean stayed at the Sunset Tower, a place that embodied the paradox of the city, a place with unmatched external beauty and a rotting interior.

Jean recalled a story of a legendary LA party. A married woman in a hot tub with several different partners. Also in the tub: her yoga teacher, a TV actress, the actress's assistant, and an infinite supply of white bakery boxes filled with birthday cupcakes. The group was found licking frosting off one another's bodies. Jean imagined the scene often with great amusement—steam rising from wet skin, mouths gaped in arousal, hair laced with sugary paste, stomachs stained with frosting.

At one of these, an acquaintance of Jean's had become so detached from her senses as to place herself in the center of a room, drunk, shrieking, and naked, and to offer any guest to take his shot—in any orifice. The men took her suggestion to heart and lined up for the excitement. The list included several notable names—stars of film, television, *and* commercials—including a man whose grandfather starred in *The Wizard of Oz* as the head munchkin.

It was stories like this, Jean had come to accept, that made LA such a strange backdrop, a frontier with a horizon that receded at pace with approaching cowboys. The most stringent of social rules applied—to beauty, status, and power—and yet could devolve into anarchy in the span of an hour. It was a city of countless laws—and none—answerable to everyone and no one.

Jean and Noelle arrived in LA just before lunchtime after a plane ride so long and so short as to feel disorienting. The hotel lobby was consistent with the city's color palette—bellboys dressed in khaki pants and lavender shirts with collars followed by a glimpse of palm at every open window. The smell of orchids slowed you down while you took in the view from the terrace: the lowlands of Hollywood sparkling like a thousand lighters.

Jean spent most of the day in her room, making calls and returning emails. She confirmed the meeting that was the reason for her visit, called her daughter on Skype, and watched her halting pixels bring them farther apart and closer together. At five o'clock, she showered and changed into jeans and a gray sweater, applied enough blush to give herself the appearance of a heartbeat, then twisted her hair into a ponytail that looked less chic than girlish. Satisfied she had done the most with her appearance, she made her way to the hotel bar to watch the lights of Hollywood begin their flirtation.

The bar was mostly empty but for a few hotel guests and aspirants, a starlet and a mogul at debatable levels of realization, an older actress and her younger lawyer, and various carnivores posing as vegans. A youngish man sat alone at the bar, looking more interested in his drink than the possibility of conversation.

Jean noticed the empty seat before it was offered—at least she thought she had when she replayed the events of the evening. But nothing she believed about that night would remain certain, including whether it had happened at all or only in her imagination.

A bald and buoyant maître d' greeted Jean and Noelle as they entered and ferried them to a wide wooden bar to wait for their table. Jean noticed the man again as she surveyed her surroundings, his shock of gray hair a welcome spark in an otherwise muted palate.

"This seat empty?"

"Yes," he said. "You can have it because I'm leaving."

"That's too bad." It was, for Jean, uncharacteristically forward.

Noelle jabbed at her friend with theatrical flourish. "What she means to say is 'thank you.' We're from New York. That's how we express appreciation."

"Me too," he said. "From New York. Also have trouble with gratitude."

Jean looked up for the first time, sizing up the stranger. His eyes conveyed a world at once. Gone was the freedom of a secret, the freedom of the pointless.

"What neighborhood?" Noelle asked.

"Brooklyn," he said. "Red Hook."

"No one lives in Red Hook," said Jean.

He paused both to look at Jean and to consider her statement. It was rare to see someone do just this, actually think before speaking. "It's true, it's very empty," he said. "That's kind of why I liked it."

Now Jean paused to think as well, to experience this bizarre human action, a simple truth shared between two perfect strangers.

They remained like this for a moment, treating small talk with import until Jean had to look away. Too much eye contact.

"What brings you to LA?" he asked.

"We're working on a movie."

"What kind?" he asked.

"An indy," said Jean.

He wrinkled his nose in confusion.

"You know. Independent films. Little stories about real people. Tend to explore the flaws of man. Take place in kitchens and bedrooms."

"The Fall of Man?"

"Flaws of man. Human nature at its truest."

Noelle jumped in to seal the gaps, to shore up the space between the stated and subtext. "Our budgets are too small for the usual movie excitement, the stuff that works best on the big screen, car chases and explosions. So we focus on what we do best. Sex and conversation. Human drama. People problems. Family, marriage, breakdowns, and breakups." Noelle did this quite a lot, finishing Jean's sentences. She viewed it as part of her job to step in when Jean needed help, when communication failed her. Only sometimes, she just made things worse. In fact, more than often.

Jean smiled at the man, who looked confused once again. She translated the translation. "We're out here, pounding the pavement."

"What's the movie about?" he asked.

"Your basic quest," said Jean. "A road trip."

Noelle interrupted again. "A girl on the road, fleeing the law, but she's really fleeing herself."

"Sounds familiar," said the man. Now he addressed Jean directly.

Jean smiled and looked away. It was the second time he had made her laugh without apparent effort. "Are you staying at the hotel?" she asked.

He nodded. "Isn't it nice here?"

"Yes," said Jean. "I always stay here. It's the only place in LA I can stomach."

Something passed between them here—Jean would remember this later—but at the time, she couldn't tell if it was the spark of lust or betrayal.

"What's the reason for your visit?" she asked.

"Also here on business."

"And you?" Jean asked. "What do you do?" She hated the sound of the question.

"I trade options."

"Stocks?" Jean asked.

"I trade the idea of stocks. But my job was replaced by a computer. So now I trade nothing with no one."

"Sorry about that." Jean raised her glass. "And congratulations."

He smiled now, surprised by Jean, surprised by his interest. "You married?" he asked.

She flinched for an instant before shaking her head. Noelle smirked and grimaced. "And you?"

He held up both of his hands, both free of constriction.

"Why not?"

"Workaholic."

"You should do something about that."

"I'm *working* on it."

From there, the flirtation escalated.

Like several things about this man, it all felt suspiciously perfect. His light green eyes, his fluid speech, his well-coifed hair, his gimlet—it all had the mark, the scent of romance, but like a replica, a parody of it even. But now, Jean was in too deep to bother with distinctions. She was brainwashed, as by a cult leader, hypnotized, as by a movie. He had her attention. And for the first time since they met, she could tell that she had his also. The mutual interest succeeded in crowding Noelle from the conversation.

Benjamin had been a broker, he explained, trading on others' predictions. He worked on Wall Street when Wall

Street still worked, when people went there looking for gold and found all manner of jackpots. Benjamin brokered deals when trades were still made by people, guessing the goals of the buyer and seller, and creating room in between for his own expectations.

Within minutes, Ben had secured his spot as Jean's new favorite person, had starred in a handful of leading roles in high-concept daydreams. But before she had reached the end of act one setup, he was ripping his bar check in half, scrawling something on the back, and handing it to her like a secret agent.

"I've really enjoyed talking," he said. "I'd love to see you next time you're out here."

Jean accepted the piece of paper.

"Give me a call if you'd like to meet. Hopefully sooner than later."

Jean smiled and nodded again, feeling slightly panicked, as tongue-tied as she had been in school receiving her first B minus. I know you already, she wanted to say. There's nothing else you can tell me. I already know you're the love of my life, that I would do anything for you. Despite the length of our acquaintance, I can already see our future: another drink, and another, winning conversation, sex too soon— and then the inevitable awkward phase, followed by friendship; and eventually the tedium, the fights, the somber, silent dinners, followed by the heartbreak, the betrayal. The only question was the ending: would they stay together?

At just this moment, the maître d' arrived with a flurry of information, announcing that their table was ready and would their guest be joining them for dinner.

"No," he said.

Jean looked down. She had hoped for more of a battle.

"Where are you headed?" asked Noelle.

"I'm headed for the desert."

"The desert?" She said it with a strange inflection, as though he had plucked the word from a list of fictional venues.

"To hike," he explained.

"Oh," said Jean.

"There are these beautiful rock formations."

"Oh," said Jean. "Well, have fun."

And with that, they walked in opposite directions, Jean and Noelle toward the table, Benjamin toward the exit.

Jean's heartbeat began to recede as she took her seat at the table. She opened the folded piece of paper and read the name he had written: Benjamin Kraft. Even the name sounded like a fictional creation.

"Don't fool yourself," said Noelle, "he's going there with a woman."

"Obviously," Jean snapped. "Obviously, I know that." But, in truth, she knew nothing at all. Benjamin had succeeded, for the moment, at emptying her brain of its contents.

As a result, when the maître d' returned to their table,

she half-expected him to announce that the gentleman had paid for her dinner.

"This man. He is a friend of yours?"

"No," said Jean. "Not exactly."

"Oh, I see."

"Why? Why do you ask?"

He looked down, then looked away, gazed purposefully out the window.

"What happened?" said Jean.

"Nothing," he said.

"What happened?" she repeated.

"I'm sure it is nothing."

"What?" said Jean.

He deepened his gaze out the window, as though he had spotted a very rare bird on a distant palm tree.

"What is it?" said Jean.

The maître d' cringed as he accepted he must answer. Then with all the flourish of a silent screen star, he leaned in to whisper. "He did not pay his bill."

"What?" said Jean.

"He did not pay his bill," he repeated.

"What?" said Jean, her pitch rising.

"I'm sure it is an accident."

"That's terrible," said Jean. "Terrible." She turned to Noelle, dreading her certain look of satisfaction, but Noelle shook her head, as if to say "don't jump to conclusions." It was too late. In the span of ten seconds, Jean had devised a narrative.

The whole thing had been a ruse, she decided, a masterful setup. She was the victim of a grift, the mark of a modern-day con man. She had been chosen, she concluded, from among the various women present not because of her beauty or charisma, but because of her innocence, the ease with which she could be swindled. And yet, even as she faced this dismal series of conclusions, her confusion was met and matched by rage, a far stronger force than suspicion.

The maître d' interrupted this maddening internal conversation. "Do you happen to have his number?" He clearly knew the answer.

Jean took a moment to make her decision. She considered the piece of paper in her pocket, pictured its handsome donor. She felt and dismissed a pang of guilt, asked herself if her doubt was disloyal. Should she hand him over just like that, or stand by this man, this stranger despite the crime he seemed to have committed? But anger—the idea that she had been duped—made up her mind for her. Her indignation was twofold, rage heightened by disappointment.

Resolved, she removed the folded piece of paper from her pocket and recited the number to the maître d' as though it were a loaded weapon.

The maître d' thanked her many times, as though apologizing for a delay in seating, then hurried across the restaurant with Jean in tow to a door marked OFFICE.

"May I see his check?" Jean asked.

The maître d' handed it over.

It affected Jean as nothing else had, convincing her that she had been duped, that she was a prank's target.

His order, a filet mignon and a Hendrick's gimlet, was clearly the favored menu of a con man.

Her heart sank farther as she listened to the maître d's side of the conversation.

"Hello, sir, I am sorry to bother you."

Followed by a short pause.

"Well, I'm sure this is an accident but you see—" Another pause. "You have left the restaurant without supplying your payment."

Jean listened, wondered now as the maître d' continued. It was the same tone, the excessive flattery of before, an amateur's interrogation. But, in this new context, the maître d' seemed somehow complicit.

"Yes, you were distracted," he said. He turned to Jean, eyes bulging. "The girl was distracting."

Jean looked down, flattered, relieved. Could this be the explanation? Had she overwhelmed this man so much that he had lost his composure, become wholly fixated on her to the exclusion of all around him?

"May I have that card," the maître d' said. "Great. Yes, thank you."

The card was procured then read.

"Thank you," he repeated. "Thank you so much." He

nodded, exhaled, a show of relief. "Yes," he said. "It was accepted."

Benjamin said something now, an apology or sniff of annoyance.

The maître d' thanked him once again, and then hung up, transaction completed.

Before the phone hit its bank, Jean began her cross-examination. "Did *he* say that?" she demanded.

"What?"

"The part about being confused?"

"Yes," said the maître d'. He headed out of the office and reentered the busy restaurant.

"Did he volunteer it or did you say it?" Jean followed behind at his heels.

"Oh," he said. "I'm not sure." He paused for a split second.

Jean watched his eyes and waited. This fact seemed crucial. Had Benjamin volunteered this as an alibi, or simply assented to the suggestion? "Did he give you a card?" Jean asked now.

"Yes, it was accepted."

"Did he seem surprised? Apologetic?"

The maître d' paused, considered, flashed Jean a look of resignation. Finally, he answered. "No, not really."

Jean nodded and smiled, all the hope that had swelled her heart officially deflated. When she looked up again, the man was gone, had disappeared into the restaurant, swallowed either by the diners themselves or the city's bottomless stomach.

It wasn't until later that night that Jean allowed herself to think about Benjamin. When she did, it had the expected effect, flooding her thoughts to the exception of all others. Finally, at 3:00 A.M., helpless to all sleep efforts, she gave into the urge and composed an abject query.

"Can't sleep. Meet for a drink?"

She deleted. Too naked.

"Hi, what are you doing right now?"

Even worse. Too open-ended.

"What's your room number?"

Still worse. Inadvertently pornographic.

"I'm in room 614."

Amazingly, even worse than the last one.

"Can't stop thinking about you."

No, of course not.

"Hi."

This was fail-proof but too banal, could lead to any outcome.

Finally, she settled on this, prizing simplicity over anything more considered.

"Having trouble sleeping. What are you doing?"

Ten minutes passed without a response, each minute adding one degree to Jean's infatuation.

"?" This was her next move, as powerful as it was desperate.

Followed by this an hour later, when she called the front desk and asked to be connected.

"Benjamin Kraft's room," she said.

"Sure thing," said the receptionist. "One moment."

One moment passed. And another.

"Sorry, we don't have a guest by that name."

"Excuse me," said Jean. "Yes, you do." She commenced a frantic spelling.

"Sorry," the receptionist repeated. Jean heard her cringe. This was not the first time she had done this, had busted someone's heart and another person's alibi in the same moment.

"You must be spelling it wrong," Jean said.

"Sorry. I've tried every K name."

"Maybe I have the last name wrong. Can you look for guests named Benjamin?"

The receptionist sighed. It was either a sigh of pity or exhaustion. Papers rustled. Computer keys tapped. "Sorry," she said. "No one."

"Oh," said Jeanie. "Oh, I see. Sorry for the trouble." She hung up, thoroughly depleted, the thrill and expectation of moments ago replaced with something different: the sinking conviction that she had fallen, not for a man, but for an empty sales pitch.

Eight

Jean battled sleep that night for hours in her hotel room. It was as though she had been visited by a real-life intruder, as though a stranger had joined her in the plush beige cell and rolled with her on the warm sheets, demanded these hours of her attention. By 5:00 A.M., Jean had considered every permutation. She had arrived, with some certainty and little satisfaction, at the following explanations:

1. Benjamin was a grifter who trolled hotel lobbies. His scam was to order a hearty meal, chat up a female patron, and then, at the moment they started to click, skip the bill and head for the highlands. His alibi was to blame his amnesia on love, her beauty for his distraction.

2. Benjamin was a smooth and seasoned playboy. His goal was to dine on filet mignon on a stranger's

kindness and then to ensure that the stranger had a reason to call him.

3. Benjamin was an international spy auditioning future collaborators. He tested the mettle of possible allies with a routine audition process, orchestrating a trial with his number as bait to see how quickly she would betray him.

4. Benjamin was an innocent man who had fallen under Jean's spell. Everything he had told her was true. His only thought in the world at that moment: when would he see her again.

5. Benjamin was the kingpin of an international cartel. His scam was much larger than steaks and gimlets; the maître d' was his accomplice. His endgame was way bigger than Jean: arms and internal organs.

6. Benjamin was a regular guy enjoying a drink after a hectic work trip. Jean had intrigued him for a moment. He had innocently forgotten his transaction. He had every intention of seeing her again until he exited the hotel lobby and she floated out of his consciousness.

At dawn, Jean prayed for the mercy of sleep, plagued by insomnia's madness. But the most damning thing about her theories and their number was the possibility that, as Jean lay in her bed, he too might launch his search, that he might sooner identify her to discover the kids and husband, to find the unflattering photos snapped at holiday parties and beach trips?

The idea filled Jean with such panic that she gave up on sleep altogether. She clicked on her light with a tug and paced the hushed hotel room. She walked to the desk, tugged at the light, and opened her laptop, heeding an impulse to jot down one final idea. Here is the fully fleshed theory that she finally accepted:

Benjamin was indeed smitten with Jean at the first meeting; the interest in his eyes had looked too real, the connection too lifelike. He had not intended to skip the bill, had indeed been distracted, but he had realized his error as he left the bar when there was still time to fix it—not a moment later. This was when he stopped and looked back, a pause Jean had noted from her table. Still, he continued on his way, allowed the error to go unnoticed. His crime was a crime of omission. He allowed the crime to be committed for him.

Somewhere around five in the morning, Jean made her final conclusion: the grifter was not a grifter per se, at least not a first degree one. He was guilty of an innocent mistake followed by a murky decision. But what was a criminal who walked into a crime, then failed to reverse it? Was he any different from a criminal who committed a crime with intention.

The same? Worse? Or better? Either way, the theory gave Jean much-needed peace and resolution. Her relief was as life-like as a real person—green eyes, shock of gray hair, inscrutable expression.

Jean checked out of the room at noon, irritable and groggy. She had spent the better part of the morning trying to sleep off insomnia but emerged at last to meet Noelle with all the trappings of a hangover: pink eyes, flat hair, skin like a crustacean, and the foggy conviction that the world outside was less reliable than the one she had slept in.

She packed her bags in a zombie's haze, still running through permutations. Her mind was the work of another force, an automated slot machine scrolling past blurry, racing symbols. The mind was horribly cruel sometimes, totally unwieldy, forbidding its owner peace at the moments it was most needed.

As the day progressed, the sting of defeat morphed into the lash of anger. Each item she packed in her suitcase—black lace bra, cream-colored thong, black shift, cashmere sweater—was another reminder of her dashed hopes. O, the lost woman.

Nine

Jean found the set somewhere between Skid Row and Main Street, in the section of the lot appropriately called "Urban Neighborhoods." The guards at the gate had waved her in after some fuss with lists and identification and Jean had wandered off, she feared, into the wrong zip code when she found herself smack dab in between the Eiffel Tower and the White House.

She knew she was back on the right track when the sky went dark, due to a satellite dish overhead large enough to exchange messages with a distant planet.

Jean paused here, trying to summon her confidence, then stepped and tripped over an electric cable the size of a jungle python.

"We're rolling," whispered a young man. He wore jean shorts and a frayed black T-shirt. He halted Jean with a hand on her arm. With the other, he circled his finger.

Jean stood still, working through her disorientation. The gesture for "rolling" on a movie set was the same as the gesture for crazy.

"Sorry," Jean whispered.

The man nodded.

They stood together in silence, his hand still on her forearm. The markings of intimacy were so clear—their proximity, their physical contact—that Jean forgot where she was for a moment and found herself thinking of her husband.

Any noise made on set while the camera was rolling, however subtle—a laugh, a cough, a sniffle—was considered anathema, tantamount to throwing mud on a master's painted canvas. Such a slip could ruin all that had been memorialized in the previous moment, exposing the camera's great lie, the illusion of perfection.

Those who endangered the shot in any way were treated without sympathy. Guests and visitors could be forgiven for such a nuisance. But a seasoned producer like Jean—she should have known better.

Jean smiled at the young man, rustled her arm slightly. He looked at her with confusion, as though he had forgotten her presence. Finally, the director called "cut" and its echo surfaced, spreading in concentric circles like ripples around a penny.

Jean smiled at the young man, a reminder and a plea. Finally, he released his grasp. She had been forgiven.

The set afforded moments like this, moments between strangers. Forty people huddled in a fanless attic, faces spotlit by klieg lights, dust floating upward like confused mosquitos. The smell of wood, mold, and musk mingled almost sweetly, the sugary taste of aspiration.

She felt it as soon as she stepped on the set, tripped over the first cable: the intangible sense of a new frequency, the presence of something electric. The circuit sped from her heart to her head, rushing in like an upper, producing the unmistakable sensation that she was part of something special.

The set could feel like a temple, the way it enforced silence. Even before the talkie was born, sound was still to be confined, doled out like gas in rations. With film, the reverence was born of respect. Film cost money; feet raced through the barrel at every second. The cost became a tenet of the religion; every frame must push for perfection.

This simple goal was understood and ingrained in every crew member. Every piece of the world must be prepped like pharaohs for embalmment, organs scooped and pickled for the next existence. This mandate—this reach for beauty—governed all behavior. Movies strove in centimeters, the control of a single rectangle. The paintbrush of the production designer, the prop guy's careful placement, the whirring brush of the makeup artist, dusting cheeks, plumping lips, spraying tendrils.

Just like this, a crew united in pious silence. The set was a space in which the dimensions demanded focus and silence, a space that conveyed the sense that you were tiny and insignificant, and yet part of something enormous and awesome.

Film retained its power just like massive, muralled churches, mesmerizing generations long after the clerics had left the building. A film could be shot on video and still feel like a revolution, just as a church could convene in a shack and form the center of a movement.

Had reverence been ingrained in man, passed on as a custom? Was the impulse to be still and silent, to kneel and rise, to whisper and yell intrinsically human? Did the same thing stir deep within your soul under vaulted ceilings? Could it happen anywhere so long as belief was clear and present?

Jean had struggled all her life to answer such questions.

Her conclusion: a good salesman could sell faith and, wherever there was faith, there was also a market.

"Jean?" A new young man emerged and gestured toward the trailer. This one was better dressed than the first; his faded and frayed T-shirt appeared to be tailored.

Jean smiled, extended her hand.

"Tim's just finishing a scene. He welcomes you to sit in his trailer or watch in video village."

The man handed Jean a pair of headphones and gestured at a table stocked with sweating cheeses.

Jean followed the young man's glance beyond the table, toward the "village." It consisted of a small clump of folding chairs scattered under a makeshift tent, a nomadic structure that could be folded and moved at the first sight of rain clouds. When weather required, the scene on set was itself floodlike, with people running in all directions, shielding electronics.

A clump of thin and fit people sat under the canvas shelter. All eyes were trained on a monitor, squinting with interest, like airport controllers waiting for approaching traffic. They seemed to be oblivious to the fact that the scene was unfolding so near to them, close enough to be witnessed in the flesh—as opposed to on a flickering television.

The residents of the village were so uniformly attractive that Jean began to wonder if they had been weighed before they were hired. Those who were not inherently beautiful were dressed to mask the difference, wearing colors that flattered their skin (gray, navy, and black), fabrics that made them look rich (silk and cashmere), and all manner of sunglasses.

Jean felt suddenly ashamed of her simple attire—a rumpled navy tunic, black tights, simple earrings—an outfit that traveled equally well on a hanger or in a wallet.

The scene appeared to involve an emotional crisis. But like so many things on set, the moment had been reduced to its fraction. Film divided action in half, preferring time in slivers, moments drawn and quartered. An action was first shot from one side, then again from the reverse angle, then again at closer range with tighter lenses.

For those watching a film being made, the effect could be

dulling. This cutting up of conversations made a study of simple action. The camera pieced out human life, dissecting the initial moment, tenderizing it like a piece of meat submitted to excessive pounding. This was the special privilege of film—to dull and then to sharpen. And yet, this endless repetition, the unrepentant boredom, was aimed to create the opposite effect: something potent, affecting, heightened.

Movies possessed that special gift reserved for superhumans: they were able to stop and lengthen time with calisthenic endurance. The camera was always hungry, an insatiable dragon, demanding its meals in digestible chunks, then ingesting slowly—one limb, one fingernail, one blink at a time—a cross section of emotion.

The wicked operation continued into the editing process, with the editor slicing up the bodies, reconfiguring gestures and parts like a demented surgeon. Only then did the cauldron's brew reveal its ingredients. The raw material of a wrapped film was made of severed humans. The editor's task was to revive a smile, a blink, a glance to the floor. And just like that, life found its better version.

Hours would pass, in rain or shine, the crew clocking the hours. Masses of people standing around, blind to bugs and boredom, all of them pressed with the same strange plan, to watch and improve time as it passed as though it were the special duty of man to preserve life on earth, to submit it to purification.

Jean found a spot in the clump and followed the gaze of the group. "What are you shooting?"

"The city is about to be bombed by an evil robot and Tim's character has ten minutes to save the planet."

Jean raised her brow in a show of reverence.

"Just fucking with you," said the guy. "Nothing much happens here. It's a transitional moment."

A walkie-talkie roared into life inches from Jean's eardrum.

"One, go to one."

"Going to one."

"Copy. Going to one," said another.

"Tim's ten-four."

"Copy that. Roger."

Jean listened closely to the rising volume of chatter. Her children sounded equally official when they played this game with empty soup cans.

"Excuse me," said the assistant.

Jean turned to find a new person at her side.

"Tim has asked me to ask that you stay out of his eye line."

"What?" asked Jean. "Excuse me?"

"He asks all visitors. He finds new faces distracting."

Jean stood in silence as she processed. "Yes, of course. So sorry," she said. "I'll try to stay hidden."

She stepped away haltingly like a genuflecting peasant, then crouched below the monitor and remained at this level for several minutes.

Finally, Jean stood and rose from her crouching position. She wandered away from the village, following an electric cable that wound its way to a massive trailer.

Several disparate groups had set up camp inside the vehicle. Each appeared to belong to its own distinct population. One group looked like executives and wore officious productive expressions. Another seemed to be dedicated to Tim's aesthetic upkeep, as evidenced by tool belts filled with brushes and scalpels. Another seemed to consist of masseuses or meditation specialists, their eyes heavy-lidded due to relaxation. And then a rung of sergeants: Tim's makeup artist, chef, and trainer.

Another group defied immediate identification: a band of jovial, fraternal men, that appeared to be personal buddies. These men filled out the better part of a large sectional sofa, where they pumped fists and joysticks in a violent video game that required them to act out a terrorist invasion.

A full kitchen gleamed behind a studded bulbed mirror, chefs and makeup artists intermingling comfortably as though they were all hard at work on the same recipe. Jean took a seat on the corner of the sofa and tried to look busy.

"Jean?" Another person in a tight T-shirt stood above her, smiling. "You hungry?" he asked.

Jean looked around, considered all possible responses. Was she obligated to accept, as with a tribal chief's peace pipe?

Would refusal be construed as rejection of this bid for allegiance?

"Tim wanted to offer you some of his personal goodies."

"His personal goodies?" Jean repeated.

"Yes," said the fit person. "Totally clean and organic."

"That's very kind. Thank you."

"He also wanted me to offer you my services." He lowered his voice in an exaggeration of discretion. "He heard you just had a baby. And he'd like to offer my services."

Jean's mouth morphed to form an oval on instinct, then widened farther into a gape of indignation.

"It'll be fun, I promise," said the man, mistaking Jean's horror for shyness.

Suddenly, the door burst open. A compact man marched into the room with the combined comportment of a leprechaun and a lieutenant.

"Wow!" he said as he entered.

The group expressed a chorus of agreement.

"Wow!" he said again.

They nodded, more heartily now although the referent was still unclear to all of them.

"Hi, I'm Jean." She extended her hand.

He nodded, as though he were coming to terms with the idea of Jean, agreeing to her existence.

The actor was older and more bloated than Jean remembered, his age accentuated by the fact that she had known him first as a teen idol. His flaccid, almost see-through skin made his face appear slightly slack, like a helium balloon three days after a birthday party. His soul seemed to have followed suit, loosening somewhat since the eighties.

Jean continued to smile blankly, hand still extended, waiting for a punch line or antecedent. Then she realized Tim was nodding at something nearby—a vat of germicidal cleanser. She scurried to lather up before making physical contact.

Tim watched, smiling broadly, as Jean sanitized. The ritual complete, he grasped her hand and pulled her toward him. "Wow," he said once again. "You're not at all what I pictured."

"Oh," said Jean. That he had pictured her seemed to be a good sign. But it raised new questions. Was she worse or better? Had she dashed or surpassed expectations?

The spectators in the room looked on with varying degrees of interest. But to Jean, the referent was becoming clear. Both Jean and Tim understood the nature of the transaction:

Tim would take a fee cut on Jean's estimable indie, making a play for renewed street cred and possible award consideration. Best case, it bolstered Tim's image, proving he was willing to take on important subjects. It sold in a flurry of offers at Sundance, deal inked on bathroom tissue, slipped into Oscar contention on a category loophole. Worst case, it got a limp release or reviews that read like hate mail, in which case Tim dismissed the experience like crumbs after dessert, throwing the director under the bus and citing creative differences. His image would revive at no great cost to him. He would lose a month of his life to an all-expense-paid vacation and get to know a new batch of attractive women.

"Wow!" Tim said.

"Yes," Jean said. She realized now this was the appropriate answer.

It was as though she had unlocked the key to their communication. "I'm looking forward to working with you on your little movie."

"We're looking forward to having you," Jean said. She indulged one use of the word she disliked. "We"? Who was she kidding? This was every man for himself.

"The film is very political," said Tim. "Quite radical, in fact."

Jean formed an affirming smile though she did not agree.

"I see it as a fable about the American dream, but the nightmare version. A man and his car. A guy and his gun. No sidekick, no crutch, no friend in the world. Just point A and point B. Trying, failing, failing some more. More trying."

Jean tried to mimic the appearance of a human connection. Widened her eyes, nodded.

"I have a few ideas," Tim said. He paused grandly.

Jean waited and, as she did, noted that everyone in the room was watching.

"I'm gonna do a walk," he explained.

Jean struggled to find the right reaction, a task that was even more difficult now that she was aware of her surveillance.

"This man has a limp," Tim said. "A bum leg. He might even be pigeon-toed."

Jean nodded.

"A shackle around one foot. An impediment. A disadvantage. He's Joe Plumber. Mr. Main Street. Uncle Sam's gimp-legged hooker."

Jean stopped nodding, concerned it would begin to seem ironic.

"Don't worry. It will be subtle," said Tim. "It's not like I'm not looking to make some statement about American politics."

Jean tried to nod again but the gesture was half-hearted. The assurance of goals he did not have only served to confirm the goals he did, just as the phrases "no worries" and "no problem," for Jean at least, raised concerns rather than dispelling them.

"You don't like it," Tim declared.

"What? No," said Jean. "It could be great."

But she had been busted. Tim was a skilled actor, which meant he could not only manufacture emotions but also read others'.

Jean did her best to assume the look and feel of enthusiasm—the rise in the brow, the mouth's gentle upturn— hopeful that the look of it would mimic its experience. "You and Sam will discuss all this," she said, eager to change the subject.

"Sure, yes, of course," said Tim. "Just wanted to let you know what I'm thinkin'."

Jean felt it happen in the span of this single sentence. He dropped his belief in Jean just as he dropped the "g" in his gerund. "It's very exciting," Jean said, conscious she was losing footing. She looked to Tim. Tim looked to her. Both were grasping, reaching. And in that moment magic died. Two acrobats fell from their trapezes.

"Wow," said Tim, "it's gonna be good."

But both now knew that whatever "it" was would likely never happen.

A member of Tim's team arrived and stationed herself near him, fluttering like a hornet.

"You need me?" Tim asked.

"Do I ever," she said.

He flashed a boyish grin.

And then, like a bursting rain cloud, a deluge of walkie-talkies.

"One, go to one."

"Going to one."

"First team is on the move."

"Roger."

"Heading into the works."

"Copy."

"Copy that," said another.

Gradually, every walkie-talkie on set confirmed its agreement.

The hornet greeted her flower.

"Guess I'm needed," Tim told Jean. "See you on set."

Jean paused, unsure if his statement was a promise or an affirmation. And before she could think to censor herself, she replied, "Will I ever!"

She regretted it as soon as she said it not only because it was corny and unlike her. But worse, because a salesman speaks in facts; she had ended with a question.

Jean watched as Tim was noiselessly ushered out of the trailer. She sat for a moment, somewhat perplexed, questioning the finality of his exit. Then, deciding that the meeting was over indeed, she gathered her belongings, certain of one thing: she would never see him again. Ever.

Ten

Home brought its own store of pressing and pleasing distractions. The kids had missed Jean horribly and Sam had made his usual botch of battening down the hatches. Laundry was piled in heaping towers that blocked entrances to bedrooms. Dishes and their bacterial spawn had begun to blossom. The children had gained a new desire to be near, next to, and on top of their mother, a desire that manifested itself in constant clawing and pawing. Jean returned the ardor with redoubled attention.

She spent the night of her return in the usual meditative posture, scouring the Internet for shreds of intrigue, companionship, and diversion. But tonight, rather than pursue her usual line of inquiry, she focused on her new subject. And it was infinitely more fruitful. It was, like all the best narratives, totally unpredictable, an exclamation point followed by a question mark, a promising beginning with any possible ending.

Jean employed her computer now with new rapacity, this time fueling not pages of odes, but rather a meticulous investigation. She was aided by all the instruments at her disposal—Google, Facebook, Twitter—and a brand-new host of sites devoted to the safe and legal discovery of public records. These included, amazingly enough, criminal history, real estate records, and the addresses of all sexual predators within a fifty-mile radius. The sites tended to advertise themselves as tools for genealogy, ways to reconnect with long-lost friends, or reconstruct your family tree.

But the friendly offers of these sites were quickly obscured by their demands, the tiered levels of access they offered, and the taunts with which they dangled new promises. These were cures for the greatest ill in the world—yearning, heartbreak, desire—all of it yours for a bargain price, if you just sign right here. Just like that, these sites sold Jean the solace she craved. Like the most skilled salesman, they defined the problem, then happily sold the cure. Like a woman, they awakened—*created*—desire, then dispensed with the very need she had inspired.

Jean, seasoned salesman that she was, fell for it hook, line, and credit card. The seller became the buyer.

The information—or rather the lack of it—came quickly at first. He was not listed on Facebook, nor member of any social network. There was no visual trace of him anywhere else—no entries for him on Google, no record of his time at school, no articles published. No photos of him at birthday parties, in the background of others' life events, no mortifying drunken snapshots from someone's summer barbecue. No, for all intents and purposes, Benjamin did not exist.

And yet, perhaps this dearth could be a clue, not an impediment. There had to be a reason for this black hole, this vortex of evidence. What person got to adulthood without leaving a footprint? Perhaps his name itself could be blamed, had obscured him in a crowd. An hour spent perusing these sites yielded some basic facts.

Benjamin R. Kraft
Aliases: Benjamin Kraft
Additional names or nicknames. For example, "Robert"
   may go by "Rob," "Bob," etc.
Age: 50
Criminal Data: [1 record available]
Birthdate: **9/16/1964**
Phone: **212-555-5000**

icon_email.gif ¬
Email Found!_- Send Message
Show Social Networks

Benjamin Kraft
J.P. Morgan

383 Madison Avenue
New York, NY 10179-0001
p: 212-555-3339
1__#$!@%!#__icon_email.gif ¬
Email Found!_ - Send Message
<u>Show Social Networks</u>

Benjamin Kraft
Pilgrim Inc.
New York, NY 10152
2__#$!@%!#__icon_email.gif ¬
Email Found!_ - Send Message
<u>Show Social Networks</u>

Benjamin Kraft
412 W 39th Street
New York, NY 10038
p: 212-555-4932
3__#$!@%!#__icon_email.gif ¬
Email Found!_ - Send Message
<u>Show Social Networks</u>

Benjamin Kraft
President and Chief Executive Officer
Radial Systems
909 Seventh Avenue
New York, NY 10049

p: 646-555-3321
4__#$!@%!#__icon_email.gif ¬
Email Found!_ - Send Message
<u>Show Social Networks</u>

Benjamin Kraft
Associate
Redding LLC
1515 Broadway
New York, NY 10115
p: 212-555-2508
5__#$!@%!#__icon_email.gif ¬
Email Found!_ - Send Message
<u>Show Social Networks</u>

James Kraft
Plumber
135 W 17th Street
New York, NY 10013
p: 212-555-2231
10__#$!@%!#__icon_email.gif ¬
Email Found!_ - Send Message
<u>Show Social Networks</u>

James Kraft
Director
Mapper Investments

109 W 90th Street
New York, NY 10024
p: 212-555-4347
11__#$!@%!#__icon_email.gif ¬
Email Found!_ - Send Message
<u>Show Social Networks</u>

Slowly, Jean began to accept a notion of Benjamin's existence, a notion whereby he said and did real things and therefore his one amoral act might be viewed as an anomaly. And still, even as this notion hardened into belief, an equally palpable feeling settled right alongside it. It was the inkling that she should stay on her toes, stay vigilant and suspicious.

The feeling was not entirely dissimilar to what one feels during courtship, the conviction that one must act quickly or else lose one's advantage, the fear that one could be disqualified for a gaffe or misstep. But here, the usual indicators of love—the wondering, the elation—were matched by their negative twins: a sense of doubt, of danger, of deception.

Was this any different, Jean asked herself, from the typical romantic jitters? Was this deception any more dubious, this mystery any more baffling, the details any more illusory, the motives any more mysterious than those between any two strangers? Indeed, for all new acquaintances, for any pair of new friends or lovers, the goal of those first deceitful words was to bring those two people together. So, of course, they can be forgiven?

Jean's research provided an outlet for these standard romantic phases—the investigation, the performance, the presentation—and a drawer in which to place her thoughts, a bookmark for her worries, a way to prevent them from cluttering her mind and its considerations. Best of all, it provided an application for Jean's greatest compulsion, a means of controlling and putting to good use incessant, unbridled thinking. That tool was, of course, also unbridled in its own measure and, like Jean's brain, alternately useful and useless, accurate and misguided. The Internet is arguably the world's best source of information on human behavior. And, any doctor will tell you this, also the source of the grossest of errors.

Anyone with a laptop knows well how the computer, just like the brain, can be the site of wrong turns and false leads. It is rife with what detectives and academics call searcher's bias. In other words, the Internet is filled with dangerous detours—the kind that cause hikers to lose their trail and send them rerouting in noonday sun, hobbling away from their tents, away from nearby lakes and rivers, instead into treacherous bear-infested mountain paths. But perhaps this is the reason people go hiking: to gamble with just these alternatives.

Unfortunately, there is no credible source, no accurate measurement of motive, no standard unit of human emotion, no way to quantify a person's plans or intentions. These things change even before they take shape, hopping like baby birds, darting away from the place they perched the moment they appeared to be cornered. Desire, intention, motivation—the words themselves are misnomers, for they imply that these things are things indeed, as opposed to passing notions. These things change from things to thoughts, then thoughts back to things again—and they change constantly and quickly, most mercilessly on those occasions when we think we know where we are going.

Just like this, Jean scaled the icy mount of human intuition, a peak that recedes ever further from the climber with every step she takes toward it. Still, she was unperturbed as she climbed, arguably even emboldened, for she was convinced, if only for now, that she could decode and define the male brain provided she did enough research. As to her own psyche, she had wandered perilously far from base camp.

Eleven

Jean's first line of questioning was to find credible sources. But lacking a fertile starting point, the traditional purview of a detective, virtual friends and neighbors, would have to suffice for references. Of course, Jean's line of inquiry was not only investigative; she had given herself to the idea that Ben was a knowable person. Her questions were more predictive, more in the line of forecasting. How would he be if they dated? What would he do after their first kiss—retreat or come forward? What would it be like to fall in love with someone so elusive? It was as though Jean were a weatherman and Benjamin an unruly system. How could she leave the house again, risk total saturation without a careful analysis of the storm's nature? And what, after all, is the good of an umbrella in a tornado?

But Jean, poor Jean, forgot the curse of every detective. There is no amount of research, no perfectly credible source that can predict human behavior. The best and only clue one has is basic intuition, tempered by the alternately accurate and misguided history of past performance. Regardless, she needed more data.

It was this feeling specifically that drove Jean to the hard-core Web sites, sites that demanded deposits, not of $49.95, but much larger intervals simply to advance from the introduction to the next level. But now she was filled with the kind of fervor that fueled shopping sprees and addictions. Her desire had crossed from wanting to needing, from coveting to craving. And her body obeyed this conversion, experiencing the need as a necessity, the craving as a compulsion—an itch that must be scratched, a question that must be answered, a magnet that requires its attraction, an animal that traverses a continent in search of a drop of water.

Just like this, Jean moved on to the professional-grade Web sites, sites that promised access to information available only at local police stations, courts of law, and the Library of Congress. Just like this, she accessed things that moments ago had eluded her—real estate records, criminal history, high school commencement date, college classmates, dormitory name, phone number, addresses, and emails, as well as the names of those who had searched before her.

There were sites that offered knowledge and its companion, context. Not only did they reveal details about the identity of the person for whom you were searching—long-lost friend or family member—but, alongside these moonlit pearls of fact, the ultimate golden nugget: the names of those with whom he had been connected.

Just like this, Benjamin's past extended out before Jean like a comet that etches its hazy trail on the blackened skylight. The Internet had collected a sample of his past—and the pasts of those who had crossed it. It was the ultimate guide for prediction. The simple push of a button, combined with determination and a couple of dollars, had uncovered an untouched cache, a man's fossilized footsteps—the schools, the driving infractions, the girlfriends.

Jean stomached two opposing feelings as she scoured the information: pride and pity. For she knew that she now knew Benjamin better than he could know himself. She was like Cassandra now, a mountaintop mystic. Her vision extended to the horizon, surveyed unseen connections. She was staring at the plot points of his life, a young man's first two acts.

Just before six, Jean gathered her things and turned off her computer. She was now convinced of two things: one, that she knew Benjamin and two, that she knew nothing. Thus persuaded, Jean pushed back at her hopes—and the force was impressive. It must have been how her daughter felt when she asked her mother about Santa, weighing the merits of her suspicions against the yield of her expectations. It took an awesome force either way to enact belief or negation, like pushing a boulder up a hill or walking in a windstorm. Thus challenged, Jean glanced out the window at the first slats of daylight and, hearing no sounds of stirring in the house, picked up the phone and dialed 911.

"This is not an emergency," Jean began. "I want to be clear about that."

"Ma'am," said the voice. "What is your address?"

"I repeat, this is not an emergency, but I have reason to believe I've been targeted by a criminal."

"Caller, what is your address?"

"I met a man in a bar when I was in California. He left without paying his bill." A pause. "Well, to be fair, he eventually paid but it might not have been an accident."

"You were out of town?"

"Yes, traveling for work."

"In what state did this occur?"

"California."

"But he paid his bill."

"Yes," said Jean.

"Oh," said the emergency worker. "Well, that's good."

"Yes," said Jean. "Yes, it is."

A pause passed, a pause that Jean recognized waking or sleeping. It was the sound of a person losing interest. "When is the last time you had contact?"

Jean paused again, cringing. "I wrote to him last night," she confessed.

"You wrote to him?"

"Yes."

"And how did he respond?"

Another pause. "He hasn't written back yet."

"Oh," said the emergency worker. "He hasn't written back yet?"

"No," Jean said. "He has not."

"Well, that's not good," said the emergency worker. "Doesn't bode well for the future."

Jean sat still for a moment, marveling at the situation. She had just been scolded and mocked by a total stranger. Of course, she knew it served her right for indulging her suspicions. And she knew she had no one to blame but herself, her own paranoia. What was she going to do? File a report? Her charge: apathy, rejection, *disinterest*? She imagined the urgent headline to come, the local paper on alert: IN BROOKLYN TONIGHT, A MAN WAS INDICTED FOR NOT RESPONDING TO A TEXT FROM A WOMAN.

Eventually, Jean hung up the phone and acknowledged the greater problem. There was a certain tension, she knew, between her fears and her desires. She was, after all, reporting the crime of the same man whose reply she awaited. But wasn't that always the way with love, this commingling of lust and terror, the two feelings inexorably linked, appearing to be as different entities when they were, in fact, one branch, two limbs, the same root system.

Finally, Jean stood from her desk in a delirious state, as amazed by her own ill-advised call as she was by her imagination. She was confronted again by the power of her mind to warp the simplest situation, the power of doubt to turn the lovely into the demented. She was marked, in a sense, not by Benjamin, but by her own perception, marked for dashed hopes for one reason: because it was her expectation. Self-loathing, she realized now, put her in the greatest harm. Self-loathing—she could feel this now—was, by far, the most devious con man.

Twelve

Jean retreated to her room a beaten and broken woman. She found Sam sitting up in bed, having regained his lust for life—and his erection.

"There you are."

"I couldn't sleep."

"What have you been doing?"

"Reading," she said. "And thinking."

"It's scary. I know," said Sam. His voice was raspy, different. "But I know you're gonna come through. I know you can do this."

"I'm really, really tired," Jean said.

Sam pressed on regardless. "I've had a realization," he said. "I've taken you for granted."

Now Jean turned to face her husband, took him in for a moment, the stripe of pink flesh near his waist in between his T-shirt and his boxers, the hungry look in his eyes like a dog at the foot of a table. Then she turned back to her dresser and continued changing into her pajamas.

"You're so sexy," said Sam. "Out there, fighting for us. You sexy, independent woman."

"Sam," said Jean. "I've been up all night. I'm going to sleep for an hour."

"Come on. Before the kids wake up." He lunged from the bed and kissed her neck, his version of romantic.

Jean returned the kiss with a polite version.

"Honey, we're really doing it," said Sam, ignoring Jean's signal.

"Doing what?" said Jean.

"Teaming up."

"Against?"

"You know . . . the People Who Said It Couldn't Be Done. The Disbelievers. The Masses."

"Honey, there's no opposing force. It's just us and our goals and compulsions."

"Jeanie, come on. This is the dream. Both of us on the same side, fighting for redemption."

Jean disengaged more forcefully now, hoping to convey a baseline of support while discouraging further advances.

But Sam misread the signal. He yanked at the covers with an invincible smile, like a magician removing a drape. Then he pulled off his shirt with an awkward tug and reclined as though he were on the Riviera.

Jean looked at Sam from above, felt a flicker of something

potent. From this angle, this man lying on his back, her husband-of-a-decade, elicited something like arousal. But arousal it wasn't.

It was the intersection of several sensations converging on the same nerve center: embarrassment, therefore pity; then anger for being made to feel sadness; then obligation, followed by dread; then anger for being responsible for his consolation.

She took a seat on the bed, attempted to harness the sensations. Then, she straddled her husband. Perhaps she could funnel this bundle of feelings into some satisfaction.

"Oh honey," said Sam.

"Oh Sam," said Jean.

"Oh honey, you're so beautiful. You're the most amazing woman."

Jean closed her eyes and tried to believe, to think herself into conviction.

"Oh Jean," said Sam.

"Oh Sam," said Jean.

"Oh baby, we're gonna do this."

And before Jean had time to reprimand Sam for the dreaded preposition, or to clarify its referent—the movie or the orgasm—she found herself overwhelmed by anger or arousal or pity and all at once this dangerous combination exploded into the bright white light of resignation.

Thirteen

In the office, Jean found herself at a loss, totally and completely useless, unable to focus on her work and unable to disengage from the grip of her investigation. Noelle could be heard in the next room, gamely pitching her heart out. Every fourth word of her conversation wafted into Jean's cubicle, creating the sense that Jean was underwater, grasping the last whispers of life before sinking to join the plankton.

"You okay?" Noelle asked during a water break.

"I'm fine," Jean lied. "Really busy."

"You're not still thinking about that guy? Why don't you just text him?"

"I might give him a call," said Jean.

"No," said Noelle. "Not a phone call. Calling is way too personal. You might as well arrive at someone's door, naked. Email maybe. *Maybe.* But email is best for work and longer personal issues. Email certainly before a phone call. And definitely text before email."

Jean sat still, considering, focused on her bobble-headed desk ornament. Was she just as futile as the rubber doll, her eager eyes doomed for delay, her endless jiggling as fruitless? "I can't shake the feeling that he might have been a valid and special person. But the moment I accept that idea, I become equally convinced that he is a serial killer."

Noelle stood, staring at Jean now with new awareness. "What's the worst that can happen?"

Jean knew the answer but couldn't bring herself to voice it. The only thing worse than losing an organ, than mutilation, swift and violent, was the possibility that Benjamin would not write back, at which point this bizarre and invigorating adventure would finally and officially be over. It was better to keep on wondering than to know this fact for certain.

Noelle stared at Jean now with unchecked pity, as though she had finally determined that Jean was beyond salvation. "Why don't you just write to the guy? That or hire a private detective."

Jean looked up, clear and revived. "Do you think they'd be listed?"

Fourteen

From: JeanieBanks@gmail.com
To: Albert Mint
  Thanks for taking my call today, and for the initial consultation. Just have to ask before we start. Is it possible he can trace our communication? Sorry. New to this.

From: Amint@mintgroup.com
To: Jean Banks
  Please send everything you know. All facts and impressions are helpful. Our communication can't be traced. Also, please send general facts he has presented to you about himself.

From: Jeanie Banks
To: Albert Mint
 His email is bkraft@mac.com. His cell is 917-555-4382. The name he gave me was Benjamin Kraft. I am sending you a long email with various facts and details.

From: Albert Mint
To: Jean Banks
 Received. We are off and running.

From: Jeanie Banks
To: Albert Mint
 Benjamin Kraft, age 36, not married, i believe his dob is 9/16/74, if
 the name is not an alias.
 mother's name is Gail Herman. She lives in San Diego.
 can't find record of a father
may have a brother or a sister.
 i believe his middle name is David
 grew up in MA
 said he went to Boston University undergrad
 has ZERO presence on Facebook, no pictures on Google, literally NO presence on the internet. very unusual.

Fifteen

That night, at her computer post, with Sam sated and children sleeping, Jean finally gave in. She could stand it no longer. She had spent enough time in a state of confusion, posing questions and pitching theories. It was time to write something that ended with a period.

"Enjoyed talking the other night. How was the desert?" She pressed Send before she could regret it.

He wrote back within thirty seconds.

"You free Tuesday?" he asked.

"Yes," she said.

"Downtown good?"

"Great," she said.

Just like that, they set the stage for the next adventure.

Sixteen

The date began like any other, with a flurry of nerves and excitement, several last-minute changes of clothes, and a frantic sprint down Lafayette in heels and then in sneakers—heels tugged back on just before she reached the destination. Benjamin was waiting at a table in the middle of the bar, requiring that she walk the length of the room in full view, an astonishing feat of self-control given that she was panting.

"I'm surprised. I have to say."

"Me too," said Jean. "I'm not exactly sure what happened."

He seemed to decide he cared about her even before she was seated. Jean felt him make this decision.

Her pulse was calmed slightly by his eyes. They conveyed a specific brightness, as though *he* were the private investigator and *she* were the person of interest.

"It's nice to see you," he declared.

"Nice to see you too." Jean took in a gulp of air, assured herself that her thoughts were hidden. Though they seemed abundantly obvious to her, Benjamin Kraft did not yet have access.

"I'm surprised," he said. "I have to admit."

This felt like a step toward her.

"I thought I had paid the bill," he said.

She shrugged, as though she was not entirely sure of his referent.

"The check at that hotel," he said. "The paper's so thin it looks like you've paid before they've actually run it."

Jean nodded once again, satisfied with the opening statements—she had not yet said anything she regretted. And she believed him already, had submitted him to a full court trial and he had been acquitted. But how could she confess her judgment so soon, offer up blanket forgiveness? How could she say that her verdict was unconditional love, that *she* was the guilty party?

"I see," she said, and shrugged again, as though she were still unsure, as though her doubt was separate from her, a cautious creature to be coaxed from the ground, a creature over which she had no jurisdiction. "It's fine," said Jean, amping up the performance of disinterest. And, for the first time in years, her performance was brilliant. She knew it as an actor feels his impact from the breathing of his audience. "I have something to confess," said Jean.

He smiled. "What is it?"

"I thought you were some kind of criminal, in cahoots with the hotel for cash, or the kingpin of a kidney cartel, running a black market."

"What did I want from you?" he asked. "Your money or your body parts?"

"Both," said Jean. "But kidneys sell for a mint, so you were willing to chop me up."

"You wanna get out of here?" he asked.

"What do you have in mind?"

"I know this great place." He smiled. "They serve internal organs."

"Already?" she said. "I thought you might be torn between my body and my brains."

"Exactly," he said. "That's for later. Right now, I just want to get you drunk."

Jean smiled. She had passed the first trial, advanced to the next level. It had been so long since she'd flirted she had nearly forgotten the mechanics. It was almost like playing a video game except the prize was pleasure.

It brought back memories for Jean, memories of a younger person. And yet, of all the dates she'd been on, all the versions of this conversation, she had never before had so much fun, and never had the facts been so open to interpretation.

When she looked up, Benjamin was scrolling through his phone, producing an array of photos.

"What are these?"

"Gorillas," he said, as though it was nothing at all, as though, these days, everyone had photos of gorillas on their iPhones.

"From where?" asked Jean.

"The Congo—darkest Africa," he said.

"Who took them?"

"I did," he said.

The pictures of primates were close enough to reveal the hairs on their heads, their dry, humanoid noses and chins, their kind, beatific expressions. The images were glossy and well-framed, the kind you might see in a nature magazine, so intimate and so much like women and men as to suggest the photographer was also a gorilla. It produced, in Jean, confusion that was, by now, quite familiar, totally in keeping with the experience of being with Benjamin.

"You went to the Congo?"

"Yup," he said.

"Are Americans even allowed?"

"They weren't for a while," he said. "But they are now."

"Why?" she asked. The question was driven by curiosity, but it came out as a demand.

"These animals are endangered. I wanted to see them before they leave the planet."

"Oh," said Jean. She nodded—mostly to convince herself.

"They were beautiful," he said. He handed the phone to Jean.

Jean accepted the phone as a gift and as evidence. Each

image was more startling than the last, each one more indis-
putably real, the opposite of Benjamin, who was, with every
passing moment, more like an apparition.

Was he a liar or a thrillseeker? A confidence man or a
cad? Or was he just a guy bragging to a girl, trying his best
at romance? It began to occur to Jean that the two things
looked exactly the same, a man trying to impress a girl and
a salesman selling his product.

But for now, Jean had lost the ability to discern between
the false and the valid—and to note that a man trying to get
a girl in bed was often indistinguishable from a pathological
liar. Just when she started to relax, to accept Benjamin as
a credible person, he said or did something that set off the
sense that she was being swindled.

Indeed, Jean experienced something odd as she scrolled
through the pictures: she grew increasingly panicked. Her
confidence—in Benjamin and in herself—began to flicker.

To be wrong, to be duped—it was Jean's greatest fear. And
as she sat in the bar, she began to feel wild and nauseous.

"Who did you go to the Congo with?"

"I went by myself," he said.

"Isn't it hard to get there?"

"No, not really."

But now, poor Jean's mind was ablaze, crackling with
questions. The urge to know objective truth overwhelmed
her entire being. Two drinks and two green eyes obscured
the fact that no such thing existed.

"What was it like over there?" she asked.

"Beautiful," he said.

She nodded, barely containing her frustration. His answer was maddeningly vague, at once sincere and evasive.

"Where else have you been that you've loved?" Jean asked.

"China," he said. "I lived there for a while. And Alaska."

"Excuse me?"

"Yup. I went on a mountain climbing trip."

"Right," said Jean. "Of course."

"Mount Blackburn, seventeen thousand feet—fifth highest peak in the United States."

Once again, the alarm flared up. Was this all an elaborate prank? Was he messing with her for sport? But how could she find out the truth without making a fool of herself?

"What were you doing there?" she said.

"Climbing," he said. "Like I said."

"And why did you choose that peak?"

"We needed a mountain you could hike in three days or less."

"We?" said Jean. She hated herself for saying it as soon as it was said. Nothing good could come of it—no way to confirm or retract.

"Friend from college. We were turning thirty and feeling lost."

Evolution's two most legible traits are surprise and contempt. One declares itself with an opening—the rise of an eyebrow, the widening of the eyes—the other occurs with a closing up, a narrowing of the eyes, a retraction of the lips. It is the look of a man on the defensive, an animal about to pounce, a man who has changed his mind, made an irreversible shift.

Jean looked up now to find Benjamin's expression changed just like this. But now she was unable to find her way, and determined to see a way out.

"You went mountain climbing in Alaska?" she repeated. "With your college friend?"

"We wanted to climb a mountain," he said. But the excitement was lost. Benjamin had turned the corner from rage to contempt, a much more powerful sentiment, and one harder to reverse.

Anger, just like lying, is a collaborative act, a pastime used to great effect to preserve pride, to enhance dignity, to avoid discomfort.

Jean nodded, heartened again. She was finding her way back, much like a hiker rejoining his trail, finding the beaten-down shrubs, the human traces. "Sounds exciting."

"Yes, it was."

"Did you use a compass?"

"GPS—and a guide. But we still almost got lost."

"How did you find your way back?" Jean asked. She may as well have been asking herself. Everything he said now tripped an alarm, causing her either to doubt Benjamin or to doubt herself.

"We almost didn't," he explained. "But the guide saw us on the trail."

"How did he see you?"

"I don't know. Guess he was on another ridge."

"He could see you from another mountain?"

"I don't know. I didn't ask. I'm not a geologist."

"You're a climber."

"I was. That day."

"You just went there? For vacation?"

"Pretty much."

Jean regretted the question as soon as she said it, not only because it failed to bring her any closer to revelation, but also because it made her seem like the liar instead of the detective.

Benjamin sat in silence now, studying his drink.

Jean tried to organize her thoughts without much success. On one hand, she suspected she had been fooled, that this was an elaborate prank. On the other, she entertained the idea that she was clinically paranoid—unable to trust the truth.

But what was truth, she asked herself, as she sat in silence now. Was truth the version of himself Benjamin presented at the bar? Was truth the tale of his upward hike, as seen from the ridge up above? Or was truth like footsteps on a climb, some to the right, some to the left, a collection of random fits and starts as traceable as wind, steps that accrued to a narrative line but only when seen from a distance?

Benjamin seemed to sense Jean's racing thoughts, and to face his own, seemed torn between the impulse to flee and to stay and enjoy the scrutiny. "I was working sixty hours a week. I had very little money or vacation, but I badly needed a change of scene and a change of perspective. So I started to look for the right mountain."

"Everest?"

"Two weeks."

"K2?"

"Over three."

"McKinley."

"One if you're lucky."

Jean sat in silence for a moment, digesting Benjamin's claims. Either way, the abundance of detail did not seem like the hallmark of a lie, but rather proof of life.

They smiled, renewed in their connection, renewed in mutual trust, tied by the thread that extends between people, as thin as a spider's silk, when interest is met with interest, when questions are met with answers, when like is met with like.

"I'm never going to see you again. Am I?" he said.

"Why do you say that?" Jean said. *I Googled you,* she wanted to say. *I found out where you live. I know your mother's maiden name, your first apartment address. I know the name of your high school, what year your father left. I've already decided on trust, turned doubt into belief. I've harnessed the absolute value of love, so that now the very doubt I felt has been converted to a disciple's faith. I know that neither one of us would think this is fruitful or fair, but I would bet my life on the fact that if you gave me a day—just a day—you might stay with me for the rest of your life.*

But she said this instead: "I don't believe you."

"What?" he said.

"I don't believe you," Jean repeated.

"Wow," he said. "That was rude."

"What's rude," said Jean, "is lying for sport."

"I don't know what to tell you," he said. "Everything I've told you is true."

Jean shook her head rhythmically, as though the act could counteract the lies, as though she could fight fire with fire, lies with her own set of facts.

"Look, I don't need to sit here while you question my integrity." The snarl again, the upturned lip, firm and asymmetrical, as though the mouth were erect.

"I think we've hit a wall," said Jean. "I'd like to get the check."

"Yes," he said, "I'd like that."

They both looked into the restaurant, as though toward a loud crash, eyes roving and necks craned in search of the nearest waiter, as though it were a competition to see who could get his attention first. Fortunately for Jean and Ben, that waiter ignored them both.

The mood recovered somewhat when Jean and Ben emerged from the bar. The sky was light in the particular way of a September evening, with people wandering in and out of the street without obvious purpose as though traffic laws had been temporarily suspended, the better to allow romance to flourish.

"So tell me about China," Jean said.

"What do you want to know?"

"Was it hard to learn the language?"

"Not really. There's no conjugation."

"No conjugation to the verb?"

"Right."

"So how do you know who's doing what?"

"Every action taken by any person has its own sound and meaning."

"Oh, I see," said Jean. But she paused, because she still didn't. "How would you say 'I like you'?"

He paused, looked Jean square in the eye. "I like you," he said.

"In Chinese," said Jean.

"_____," he said.

"Oh." She nodded. She stood very still, watching his mouth, which was still also. It had flattened from the snarl of contempt to something more curious, as though he were trying to figure out whether Jean was a verb or an object.

They landed at a Brooklyn restaurant and sat side by side at the bar because, Ben said, sitting across from each other felt too much like a first date and just seemed easier on those who were clearly socially awkward. They struggled over what to order so long as to annoy the waiter and, when the food finally arrived, they drank more than they ate and spent the rest of the meal making each other laugh with great purpose, and finding excuses to touch by accident.

After dinner, they toppled into a cab with the usual pretenses—they would drop Ben off first because he lived closest. Jean let Ben commandeer the cab for the first leg of the carpool.

The cab slowed down on a serene and silent block in Red Hook. Trees canopied overhead. Bricks looked black under streetlights. They exchanged a warm, halting embrace and Benjamin stepped onto the sidewalk. Then he smiled triumphantly and held out a hand—either to wave goodbye or to beckon. Jean didn't wait to decide which one.

She handed a wad of bills to the driver and followed Ben up the stoop, then up three flights to the top floor of his brownstone. Ben led her to a humble and lovely apartment, a nook that would surely be described by a Realtor during the day as "sunlit." It was a claim Jean felt it could support even in the darkness as the apartment was filled with an

odd blue light particular to moonlight, its details patently
visible since the apartment had nothing in it.

"Wow," said Jean.

As soon as Jean walked in the door, she was overcome
with laughter.

"What?" Ben said.

"What?" Jean repeated.

"Yes, what?" he said.

"You don't have any furniture!"

"So?"

"The only people who have no furniture are spies or serial killers."

"I moved recently." He shrugged. "I wanted to downsize."

"In any normal situation, this would be when the girl
runs out. But weirdly," said Jean, "for the first time all night,
I totally understand you."

He smiled, perhaps the first truly guileless smile of the
night. "Really? Please tell me what makes sense," he said,
"because I'm at a loss."

"You're a total fuck-up," said Jean, "but a really decent
person. I thought you were some exotic breed, but you're
actually the most familiar version. You're a garden-variety
single guy, a commitment-phobe, a bachelor, and this right
here is your latest escape, your latest safe house. Let me
guess, you just broke up with some girl you spent the last
seven years with. She's waiting for you to 'figure things out.'

You're taking some time to find yourself, surf in Montauk, travel. It finally fits the same narrative. The most universal story of all, a man on a quest, fleeing the law, but he's really fleeing himself."

Benjamin nodded the way people nod when listening to a sermon, or as a defendant when the judge delivers a fair verdict. His face had the odd and specific look of someone feeling known and accepted.

Elated, Jean kicked off her shoes as though it were her own home. She walked across the room and sat down on the floor next to the bookshelf. She removed the first book that caught her eye and began to read out loud. She was, by now, three or four drinks past her sensible limit. But while this did its part to compromise her balance and judgment, it made for a very rousing reading. Both Benjamin and his cat stretched out to listen. The cat, an overweight hairy thing, even more unfriendly than the average feline, walked directly to Jean, passing on the right, then the left, then took a seat on her lap.

"That's weird," said Jean.

"What?" asked Ben.

"I'm not a cat person."

"It *is* strange," he agreed. "She doesn't like anyone."

It was here that Jean finally dropped her doubts about Benjamin. The thing that was technically most bizarre— this barren spy's apartment—was the thing that endeared her to him most. He was just a confused boy with familiar damage, a man disassembling his life, determined to learn the difference between love and happiness.

The kissing that night was rushed and fun and wild in the best possible way, fueled by the fear of two people who don't know if they'll see each other again. It was fear, this open question that powered the night for both. They made out for what seemed like hours before their clothes came off.

But like so many great memories, it evaporated fast. Had she gripped his back too hard? Had he kissed her neck? Had the sponsor of the night been love itself, because it was there in that bed, or because he took control of her body and used it for himself?

Had he felt any or all of these things? That night or sometime the next day? Or was she one of a hundred girls, eclipsed by the sunrise, the truth of what happened as dead and alive as a photograph? She let herself out of the house at five before she could find out.

Seventeen

The morning after is always defined by the night before—insofar as the night before can be accurately remembered. For Jean, the new day was a chance to relive, to organize her thoughts, to memorize the words and gestures of the night, as though they could be written and understood, used as a valid predictor. Of course, she knew that nothing was binding, not even when inked and signed. And yet, she found herself ratcheted up, all but shaking her phone to generate the message she awaited.

By one, Jean was somewhat concerned. By two, she was despondent. By three, she was in a rage. By five, despair again. Her perception of the evening had undergone a shift, beginning with the clarity of promise, followed by the blur of dashed hopes. It was a dangerous place from which to begin a new correspondence.

She sent a message to Noelle, conscious she was reaching the zone in which she committed acts of self-destruction.

"Do I have to wait for his text?" she wrote.

"What time did you leave the apartment?"

"Around five," Jean said.

"Then yes. Absolutely."

Jean weighed Noelle's advice against her desired decision. "Why?" wrote Jean. "What's the problem with honest communication? I thought that was what phones were for."

"Phones are weapons," Noelle wrote back, "instruments of torture. Silence is your only option. Any word, regardless of what you write, reeks of desperation. The simple act of writing is a loss of power, implying that he is on your mind at a point when you may be far from his thoughts."

"But why should I perpetuate this arcane power dynamic?"

"Because you're playing a game," wrote Noelle, "in which men are the opponent. Men are, by nature, hunters. They only want what they must capture."

"I don't accept these gender rules. I don't think they're innate. I think they're imagined."

"They're facts," said Noelle. "Ingrained over generations. Far older than the technology at your disposal."

"I don't see why I should conspire with my own subjugation."

"You seem determined to write," said Noelle. "Just keep it brief if you do. And try not to forfeit all of your power. Remember, the best sellers don't ask. They offer."

"Right," said Jean. "Thanks."

"Keep it to three words or less. As though you're insanely

busy. And don't use a period at the end. That's how busy you are. You don't even have time for punctuation."

Satisfied with this mandate, Jean geared up for her missive.

"That was fun," she began. This seemed short and sweet. It assumed a kind of power, made her the judge of the night, not its guilty defendant. But it was lewd, she decided, and deleted.

"That was fun," she tried now. "Sorry I was suspicious." What this lacked in bravado, it seemed to gain in candor. She pressed Send before she could second-guess its wisdom.

Thirty seconds passed, bringing Jean close to madness, compelling her to add a second phrase, as though she were simply expanding upon the first, as though it had always been intended.

"You are smart and hilarious and a very good kisser. Still, given everything, I think we should put last night in the past and skip right to the friend part."

This time, he replied within thirty seconds. "You're pretty great yourself." And then: "I would love to have you as a friend!" which put the nail in the coffin.

"Great!" Jean wrote. The exclamation point was a necessary retaliation, a dagger directed at her own heart. Just like that, Jean birthed and killed the first flutters of passion.

Eighteen

From: Albert Mint
To: Jean Banks
Jean,

Sorry for the delay. I have some findings which may be of interest.

Our work seems to confirm what he has told you about himself, and we've found no criminal record or other indication of questionable conduct. We can keep digging, but here are some rough notes on the project.

Benjamin Kraft, age 36, was born on September 16, 1974.

It appears that he is currently employed with Mapper Trading Inc. There have been no disciplinary actions filed against him.

Several online sources indicated that he received a BA from Boston University, which is supported anecdotally by the fact that several of his past addresses are located on or near the university campus.

We found no record of any criminal cases (felonies or misdemeanors). This included a state-wide criminal records search in New York and onsite criminal record searches in Montgomery County, MA, and Bronx County, NY.

Kraft's mother is Rachel Herman. Rachel, age 68, was born on April 26, 1943. Rachel lives at 1378 Eustace Street, Belmont, MA, according to databases.

As you saw, Kraft does not have too much of a presence online. The few references we found related to his previous places of employment.

Looking forward to your thoughts, and hoping it's helpful.

Albert

From: Jean Banks
To: Albert Mint
Albert,

I sincerely appreciate your taking the time to find and send this information. I now feel extremely foolish for pursuing my suspicion. But I was unable to put my mind to rest given the abundance of odd details and the startling constellation of coincidence. Thanks for taking it to heart and for being so thorough.

I think you put it best when you said PI firms should

be on every corner, like accountants or real estate bro-
kers. There's no forum in which to allay one's fears
about a stranger, and this makes us vulnerable to two
things: the stranger and our imaginations. But I think
I've discovered one thing worse than vulnerability: the
power of self-doubt to distort the truth, to change not
only one's perception, but also the outcome.

Thanks again.

Jean

From: Albert Mint
To: Jean Banks
Jean,

Thanks for your thoughtful note. I'm happy I could
be of service. I hope you have no regrets. I have found,
in my experience, that people's instincts are always
valid, even if the exact nature of their beliefs lacks ac-
curacy and specifics. I caution you never to discount
what you are thinking. Things imagined are just as
legitimate as things that are real—at least in the business of human character.

Albert

Jean received Albert's note with a mixture of relief and
sadness. The distance between the two feelings made for a
startling sensation. It stung in the same way as a shock, an
electrical impulse, the same way combining hot and cold

water produces two disparate effects before becoming something new with its own temperature. The confirmation that Benjamin was a valid and honest human was eclipsed by the dawning fear that she alone—her doubt and suspicion—had killed their chances. It was as though she had spent her life devoted to animal preservation then awoken one day to find herself face-to-face with a white and foaming tiger, forced to shoot her favorite creature.

She stood from her desk and approached the door, shoes and jacket on, then turned and retreated to her bedroom, where she attempted a live burial under pillows and blankets. Lacking a working social compass, she was loath to trust any of her instincts. Seemed best to lock herself in her room and spend some time in silence. The worst villain, Jean realized now, is the one that attacks from within. Sadly for Jean, she was stuck with herself for the foreseeable future.

Nineteen

Like most of life's best story lines, the emails began as a joke. Sam knew Jean was flirting with Doug and wanted to make a point. He had not yet stooped to full-on snooping. No hacking or illegal activity. Just casual glances at her computer when she was out of the room and the occasional abduction of her phone into a locked bathroom. At the sink, he would scroll through the neon screen while Jean roamed the house until her calls for him grew so loud that he had no choice but to open the door and deposit her phone on a random shelf.

It was clear to Sam, from his limited view, that Doug and Jean were in touch. How could he know that this archive had not actually been transmitted? And that the bulk of her transgression had transpired with another person? Of course, it didn't matter whether or not they had been received. His wife was in love with another man, felt things for another person, and this alone was enough to spur both rage and recrimination.

What was unclear was the degree of guilt, the quality of her betrayal. Still, it was not pure jealousy that compelled Sam to act. The little he had read of Jean's emails made Doug seem like an insufferable twerp. That Jean had been charmed—and spurned—by him called her judgment into question and constituted a second rejection.

The first email was a simple prank, a dare to himself: a note from a female fan, praising Doug's last book. He wrote it from a new account, which he struggled to name. He finally decided on MmeRoault97@yahoo.com. Madame Bovary's maiden name seemed a fitting tag.

Sam enjoyed the exercise more than he expected. Writing from a secret perch, professing his love in an epistle, posing as a young girl, writing a note to another man, a man obsessed with his woman. Writing from a secret account, forming an avatar on a computer, writing as a man, playing a woman, to a man—it was thoroughly modern, and somehow very old-fashioned.

He waited for a response with all the anticipation of a suitor, checking his email at ten-minute intervals, tapping the refresh button. When Doug wrote back, Sam had already scripted his response, and struggled to revise it according to the new information. It was just this weird compulsion that made Sam a good writer: he was dead set on his script—sometimes to the exclusion of his characters.

"Dear Emma," Doug wrote back. "You're far too kind to this humble writer. You see I am but a mere guy, one plagued by all the pitfalls of the male character. My books are really an apology to all of you better creatures, my way of saying, 'Hey, cut us some slack. We're just trying to keep our heads above water.' That said, I accept your praise gratefully and muse at my own good fortune to have struck a chord in such a fine reader."

Doug signed off without a more explicit solicitation. But any woman—and even a man playing a woman—knew his email was clicks away from an invitation. Sam read the letter with equal parts delight and revulsion. The glee was almost too much to bear email's Pavlovian pleasure, and the success of his deception.

There were other aspects to the dialog that Sam enjoyed. Doug's humiliation was sweet—the ease with which he lapped up the praise, the speed of his reversal, the vanity, the pretense. And yet, Sam couldn't help harboring a distinct admiration. He too had struck this very tone in past messages to women. And though it made his stomach churn to imagine his own wife as a reader, he couldn't resist falling prey himself both to the game and the conversation.

Sam sat on Doug's response for the appropriate time. Years of actual courtship had taught him the going rate: a multiple of two on the previous writer's response time. But now he faced a greater debate: would he take this to the next stage, from pen pal to face-to-face interaction? Would he be content with the knowledge that Doug was so easilly fetted? Or would he push on to the next step, seek higher levels of humiliation? For Sam, there was no contest. He was already hooked. For even a man playing a woman writing to a man could not resist the challenge.

"Dear Doug," he wrote. "Everything you say is more amazing than the last. Forgive me for being so forward, but can we meet in person?"

Sam reread the note several times before pressing Send. He had upped the ante in an irreversible way, and now had only to wait to see if Doug accepted. But once you've begun to gamble, the ante has no limit. The ante rises with the desire to play, if not one's ability to triumph.

Sam waited now with new fervor. He had two things at stake: Doug's humiliation and his discovery, evidence he would share with Jean at the first possible moment (should Doug submit to the entrapment and prove that he would hop into bed with the first fawning woman). Luckily, Sam had not long to wait. Doug was an easy target. He took Emma's bait like a fish in a lake and pushed it yet further.

"It's not fair that you've read my work, and I have not read yours. I'll make you a deal. This seems only fair. You show me something first."

Sam had reached a crucial juncture in the budding romance. He was torn between outing Doug and getting better acquainted. The hard part was—and this required a feat of self-awareness—admitting that he enjoyed both aspects. The question was which was more precious: the sting or the seduction? He hazarded one more note to Doug, conscious that he already had what he needed. He found the photo easily at www.facebookforadults.com.

Sam's pulse reached his neck when this one cleared his in-box. He had always known on principle that a man was an easy target, but had never imagined that he could, in the span of one week, land himself a pen pal and a playmate. There was as yet one unnamed feature to the sensation. Sam or Emma—he could not tell which—was decidedly aroused by Emma's picture. It was almost like a third party an actual woman was present. Sam had no choice. Full of shame and fear—themselves potent aphrodisiacs also—he stood from the computer and relieved himself in the bathroom.

This time, when Sam composed his note, he did so without a writer's flourish.

"Dear Doug," he wrote. "Get in touch with my wife again and I'll come to your house."

Needless to say, Doug did not take well to Emma's last epistle.

Twenty

The next few weeks proceeded as Jean had come to expect, with Sam in various degrees of anger and Jean in various stages of self-contempt. She woke most days in a panicked state, feeling, depending on the weather outside, further or closer to death. The first few moments of consciousness were difficult to bear. It was as though her brain were filled with sludge, as though sadness were not an absence of pleasure but a surplus of something toxic. Her only recourse was to try to distance herself from herself, to greet her thoughts as though they were distinct, and to try to influence their progress.

The first few thoughts streamed in without danger or distress, a snippet relived from work, a passage from an article she had read. And then, without fail, without mercy, the unstoppable advance—first as an idea, then as a name, then as an image—until it was all she could do to think any other thought.

To Jean's great surprise, her phone lit up before she could commit any act of self-destruction.

"Want to do something tonight?"

Jean stared at the text in amazement. Had it been an act of telepathy, two people connected across constellations? Had she willed this to happen, manifested a wish across the digital landscape? Had she made an offer he couldn't resist, dangled a question that had to be answered, incited, simply by being herself, the most mysterious phenomenon in the world, the magic of human interest? O, the phone, the sweet sweet phone, sweet messenger of salvation.

"Cool," she wrote. Then deleted. She was too old for this lingo.

"Perfect," she tried. But this was too much. Too easy, too affirmative.

"Sounds good." Did this translate over text? Or seem overly earnest?

"Great." But this seemed too banal for a lover of language.

"Sure," she wrote. The best plots towed the line between words and action.

Twenty-one

The air was warm for an October night, matching Jean's sense of excitement, creating the sense that someone had her arm, was guiding her toward her destination. She saw him standing in the lobby as she reached the theater.

"This movie supposed to be good?" he asked.

"No," said Jean. "Not really."

"Oh well," he said. "Doesn't matter. It's a good excuse to see you."

"What are you in the mood for?" he asked. "High-brow or low-brow?"

"Low," Jean said.

He seemed relieved by the choice. He picked up his pace on Sixth Avenue and Jean struggled to keep up. They landed at a Japanese restaurant, the type of place businessmen came for lunch.

Jean took a seat in the booth, enjoyed the sound of clothes

on vinyl, decided to try a new approach—honest unguarded communication.

"So where are your parents from?" Jean asked.

"The Midwest," said Benjamin.

"Right. I meant before that," she said. "Where did they come from?"

"Somewhere in Eastern Europe," he said. "Poland. Or Lithuania."

"Mine too," said Jean.

"What was their name?"

"Kraschov," he said.

"Kraschov?" she repeated.

"And then they made it—"

"Kraft," she said, finishing his sentence.

He nodded. "That's correct, Jeanie Banks."

"You know my last name," Jean went on. "But you never asked me."

He nodded, but didn't say yes.

"*How* do you know?"

"You told me," he said.

"No," she said. "I did not."

"Of course you did. When we met."

"No," Jean pressed. "I didn't."

He paused for a moment, caught in a fib, debating the best exit. "So?"

"So how do you know it?" Jean said.

"I don't," said Benjamin.

"Just say it."

"Say what?"

"Admit that you looked it up."

He straightened his back. "What is this about?"

"What is what about?"

"This questioning, this interrogation."

"I don't know," Jean said. She looked away. "I guess I just want to know that you've thought about me. That I've crossed your mind in the meantime."

He paused. It was a beautiful pause, the kind you would write into a book.

The rest of the night proceeded with a new level of comfort with Benjamin confiding in Jean while Jean provided honest advice on various subjects. An hour passed like this, without awareness or self-consciousness: two people trading fears and secrets without guile or weakness as though to prove that all human hearts were made of the same substance.

They entered the cab and Jean made her usual mistake, trading ambiguity for directness.

"How do you feel about me?" she asked. She inflected her voice with cheerful ease, as though she had not just laid herself bare, asked to be drawn and quartered.

"I don't know," he said.

"You don't *know?*"

"Yeah. I don't know yet."

"We've known each other for over a month."

"Look, you're putting me on the spot."

"Isn't that what people do? Isn't that the point?"

"Of what?"

"Putting each other on spots."

"What spots?" he asked. "What spots?"

"The ones in your life, the room we make for things that are important."

"Oh," he said. He seemed to accept this as fact. Then, seemed to reject it again. "The point of what?"

"You know. Dating, getting to know each other, human relationships."

"I thought the point was to spend time together, not to take its measurement."

"People want to know what they're doing in relation to others. That their perceptions of the world match up."

"You can't really prove perception," he said.

"Of course not," Jean said.

"And you can't really measure it."

"No," Jean said. "You can't measure it."

"And sometimes when you try, you end up changing it."

"You're being very literal," Jean said.

"Human relationships are not literal. They live in ambiguity. In between what is said and not said. In the subtext. And they lose their power as soon as you try to define them."

Jean considered this for a moment. There were merits to his logic. Then, remembering, she said, "This is starting to seem like diversion."

"Well, I can tell you this much," Benjamin said, drawing in a sharp breath. "The more you ask these questions, the less I want to answer. Everything in life is subject to interpretation. That's the fun of communication."

Jean took this as her cue to disengage. She had met her conversational match. She would not win this argument.

"I thought you wanted to be friends."

"I did," she said. "I do."

"So why do you want it to go here? It's the fastest way to ruin a friendship."

"I don't know." Jean paused. She was losing track, getting lost in his proof. "I guess because I think you're great. I have since the first day we met."

"Well, this is news to me," he said.

"I thought it was obvious."

"You think I'm great?"

"Look, don't milk it now," Jean said.

"You said it. Do you or not?"

"I told you I think you're pretty great."

"Pretty great?"

"Fine," she said. "Amazing. Do you want me to make a fool of myself?"

"No," he said. "I do not. Since when is expressing emotion foolish? It's the bravest thing a person can do."

But Jean knew that, in this case, emotion was just another pitch. She was lobbing an offer into the world, an offer that could be refused, except in this case, that offer was not make-believe; that offer was her. As far as humiliation was concerned, there was no faster route.

"I'm trying really hard not to kiss you right now," he said.

"What?" she said. "Why not?"

"Because."

"Because what?"

"Just because."

"Because what?"

"Because I have a girlfriend," he said.

"Why didn't you tell me sooner?" Jean asked.

"The same reason you didn't tell me about your kids and husband."

Twenty-two

From: Jean Banks

To: Albert Mint

Albert,

Thanks for checking in. Everything is fine. It has developed into an utterly benign situation from a personal safety perspective. And an utterly dangerous situation from the perspective of my heart. Thanks again for your help.

Jean

Twenty-three

And so what began as a random fluke settled into a habit, a part of Jean's life she craved as much as her morning coffee. Jean and Ben would meet every few days for dinner or a bike ride, making a foreign country of New York, inventing a series of local adventures. In Flushing, they ate real Chinese food. In Coney Island, they had shellfish on the boardwalk. They rode along Kent Avenue from Brooklyn to Queens, past the warehouses and row houses, past the Orthodox Jews and hipsters, in the silver light of the East River. They might as well have been hiking Everest, trekking through Asia; when Jean was with Ben, the world, the light—everything looked different.

"Here's to friendship," Benjamin said when they landed in a bar in an abandoned corner of Greenpoint.

Jean rolled her eyes. "Here's to our bizarre social experiment," she said.

And the two raised their glasses and clinked with all the hope of death row prisoners.

Sometimes, they abandoned their search for adventure for the opposite pursuit, opposite of all this movement: furniture for Ben's apartment. They must have viewed every table and sofa in New York City—midcentury beauties in walnut and pine slouching sofas in benches made from peeling leather, planks reclaimed from schools and churches. But every time they came close to making a deal, Benjamin stalled at the end, forcing Jean to reaffirm her fear about Ben and commitment and to consider that she might have to make the choice for him.

Afterward, they walked their bikes to the edge of the East River, and stared at the skyline of New York, its black and yellow carcass host to the battle between summer and winter.

"Why do you think people go nuts for skylines and sunsets?" Jean said.

"Because they have a simple narrative. Beginning and end. Renewal."

They paused, soaked in the moment, its banality and its importance.

"Maybe for the same reason people like music. Because it hits the nerve of your soul. Because the pleasure is overwhelming."

Jean paused and considered this, admired the poetry of the sentiment.

"Remember that thing I told you? About the Chinese language."

"Tell me again," Jean said.

"There's no conjugation," said Ben. "Just an abundance of words."

"No conjugation?"

"Not like Romance languages."

Jean paused.

"It's I. Want. You," he said.

She nodded.

"And You. Want. Me," he said.

She smiled.

"I want. You want. He want. She want. All of you want. We want. They want."

"Right," said Jean. "I see."

"And then there are complex phrases, whole stories comprised in a word. Same thing with skylines and sunsets. Everyone knows the story."

Jean smiled, looked down.

"I wish you would pick one for me," he said.

"Pick what?" said Jean.

"A table."

"You say that but then you'd be mad because the search would be over."

"I'd have new things to search for," said Ben. "Like a rug and a cutting board and a sofa."

"Yes, but you would change your mind. You would get bored of the table. And rather than store it in the closet, you would leave it out on the sidewalk."

"Everyone feels that way about permanent decisions."

"Yes," said Jean. "That's true. But most people learn to live with them. Those who prefer indecision . . . they like to keep their options open."

Ben nodded in a way that seemed to signify comprehension. But like so many things about Ben, what looked like one thing was not that thing, but something altogether different.

They got back on their bikes and rode for a while in the cooling sunset, then locked up their bikes and fell into a bar to have the real conversation.

"Okay, your day, by the hour," said Ben.

She complied and listed her schedule, item by item. "Wake up. Drooling and gutted. Dress kids, barely conscious. Drop kids off, ten minutes late for school. Punch clock. Pitch my heart out. Work out. Rush home. Wrestle kids to bed. Repeat ad infinitum."

"Okay, your childhood in twenty-five hundred words."

She enumerated the highlights—swing sets, first love, high school dances.

"Now list all the ways you are nuts," he said.

"In any order?"

"Worst to most normal. Here, I'll go first. Suicidal."

"Often?"

"Almost always."

"Bipolar?"

"Maybe."

"Disloyal?"

"Sometimes."

"Emotional?"

"Numb to the point of being pathological."

Just like this, they agreed on a working definition of one another, building up the trust of friends and the knowledge of lovers. Unfortunately, trust is a weak predictor of future behavior.

"Do you want to go on a trip with me?" asked Ben.

"Where?"

"Anywhere within twelve hours."

"Something about this sounds like a bluff."

"It's not. It's a real invitation."

He made a strange, determined face, pursing his lips like a raisin. "Listen, I'm very serious and I want you to listen. I have ten days of vacation and I want to go somewhere amazing. Will you come with me?"

Jean paused, met his gaze, as though she could glean the exact amount of his volition.

"You have until Friday to decide," he said. "That's when I'm buying the tickets."

She remained immobile where she was, baffled by the suggestion. Was "yes" a trap she must avoid that would betray her weakness? Or was "yes" the key to his heart, the things she craved most: true intimacy with this man, and, with him, an adventure?

The questions in Jean's mind increased to a maddening murmur until it was all she could do to sit still, all she could do to keep from talking. She tried to funnel the energy into fidgeting and finger tapping, until she sat on the edge of her stool, fumbling with the hem of her dress as though she was sitting by a pool, waiting for her chance to peel off her clothes and dive in.

"Do you like this dress?" she asked.

"Yes," he said. "Very much."

"Do you like this one better?" She pulled a different dress from her bag, the same one she had rejected an hour before then stuffed into her bag at the last minute. She felt and fought an irrepressible urge to switch one with the other and before she could stop herself, she was replacing one dress with the other in an impressive feat of sleight-of-hand and hand-eye coordination.

"Did you just change your dress," he asked, "in the middle of a bar full of people?"

"Yes," she said. "Do you like this one better?"

"Actually, yes. Much."

"How come?" Jean asked.

"I don't know. Now I can see more of you."

"Good to know," said Jean. "Didn't realize they had such different impacts."

" I he other one looked nice," he said, "but this one makes me want to rip off your clothes and fuck you in the bathroom."

"Really?" said Jean.

"Yes," he said.

"You have quite an imagination."

And before she could second-guess herself or the involuntary action, she was following him across the bar, at a twentysecond interval, into a particularly seedy and exceedingly large private bathroom. Sex itself was only one of the night's inherent pleasures—among them the gruesome greenish lighting, abundant mirrors and reflections, the silly, deformed expressions—delight, rapture, effort. The feel of his hands, the feel of his tongue, and the desperate rush with which he pushed her against the wall and peeked forced himself inside her. Thus, even after he withdrew and fell upon her, panting and sated, neither one noticed the additional release of two or three dogged little fellows that were currently swimming their way to the land of permanent and irreversible decisions, not to mention all sorts of required furniture.

Twenty-four

Jean dismissed the thought of the trip until the next morning when she had time to relive the night, to commit the
moments to memory as though filing a series of snapshots.
Only then, when it was mentally recorded, could she con-
ceive of it as a reality. She spent the next several days rumi-
nating on the subject, and wondering what happens when
you accept an invitation from a person like Benjamin. Does
he meet you at the airport on time, bags packed, ticket extended, or did he change his mind and flee, weighed down
by the pressure of acceptance?

She imagined all manner of hotel rooms, from luxe bou-
doirs to aging youth hostels, their pastel walls chipping and
faded, a damp breeze blowing in from the beach, making
sails out of the curtains. In each of these rooms around the
world that Jean dared to imagine—one in Cuba, one in
Kenya, one in China—the night ended in the same way, with

Benjamin folding her into bed, with Benjamin hitting the nerve of Jean's soul, finding something better.

Needless to say, the fantasy flourished. By Tuesday, Jean was looking at flights. By Wednesday, she was reading guidebooks. By Thursday, she was scanning hotel rooms. By Friday, she was booking tickets. And by that afternoon, she had all but pressed Send, accepting the invitation.

"I'll come."

But he didn't respond for seconds then minutes then hours and when he did, he acted like Jean had just suggested a space voyage. "I think you should go to Portland. Or somewhere in the Dalmatians."

"I should go??" Jean wrote back. "You invited me on a trip. Remember?"

The pace of the communication accelerated.

"I'm having a very bad week," he wrote. "It's been really awful. I'm leaving for Costa Rica at six. Come on down if you want to."

"Maybe I will," Jean replied.

The sun set and rose before he responded.

Now Jean felt nauseous with rage and felt compelled to convey it. The question was which was the best recourse: abject fury, soft-spoken guilt, or the same gentle reprimands she used with her children.

"I don't like the way you're treating me," she wrote. "You're not being a very nice person. Your false promises make me feel like shit. I am clear and reliable with you always."

"Sorry. Just really need this right now. My own adventure."

Jean kicked herself for her last text, for revealing such naked yearning. In a sense, hers had been a bluff as well, a test of her guess that he would back out and he had confirmed it. Just like this, Jean closed the book on Ben. First impressions reigned supreme: she should have trusted her instincts.

The first few pages revealed the ending.

Twenty-five

hey,

i hope your trip was good and that you're feeling better. sounds like the days before you left were kind of a bummer.

i've thought of you these past two weeks with sadness and confusion. it threw me that you'd leave like that— pressed some familiar buttons—excluding the whole invitation fiasco, which perhaps is best understood as a bluff on both of our parts.

i do my best to be the kind of person who listens and i have a good understanding of damaged, tortured people. i get the claustrophobia, the way it sets in within seconds. i get the way you can want one person then actually start to loathe him. i understand what it is to have two people provide different and necessary fulfill- ment, and i know what it means when a man invites you to go to an amazing place then regrets that invitation the moment you accept it.

this relationship goes one of two ways from this point forward—one, we treat each other with trust or two, we convince each other that the problem was the timing. the latter is what we will tell ourselves to make ourselves feel better.

Jean

Twenty-six

Jean knew the morning after, the same way you know you are getting a cold, with a subtle but unmistakable premonition of pain to come. She knew from the odd, silvery sheen of the clouds outside her window. She knew from the watery feeling in her throat, the hum in her stomach, that the world had changed in a distinct way since the previous evening.

It had been a decision, of course, to follow him into the bathroom. And now she would face another choice with far more stark consequences. Now, as Jean sat up in bed, she thought about movies, the way actors look when they're alone in their rooms, when they're making important decisions, how they stare into mirrors and sit on their beds nodding, brows furrowed.

Finally, Jean stood from the bed and began her morning ritual, determined to defeat her balance and her mounting anxiety. At the mirror, she began the awkward project of eyeliner application, pulling one eyelid toward her chin and exposing a veiny eyeball.

"Why are you drawing on your face?" asked Jane. She stood at the door to the bathroom.

"I'm not," said Jean. "It's makeup."

"You're putting a pencil in your eye," said Jane. "You told me not to do that."

"It's not a pencil, sweetheart," said Jean. She drew her eyelid farther down, causing one eye to pop like a ghoul.

"Yes, it is," said her daughter.

"It's eyeliner," said Jean. "Makeup."

"I want to try," said Jane.

"I'll show you one day. But you don't need it." Jean drew the pencil across her lid with discernible effort, the whites of her eyes contrasted by the red of the blood vessels.

"But why are you drawing on yourself?"

Jean exhaled. She released her lid and turned to face her daughter, trading the mirror's reflection for one that was more forceful. "Sometimes grown-ups want to make things better. To enhance, just like you do with your artwork."

"Enhance," said Jane.

"Yes," said Jean. "Add. Or improve. Or make changes."

"Oh," said Jane. She nodded. "That's usually when I mess up my pictures."

Jean sighed. Why was her daughter always speaking to

her in code? She turned back to the mirror. "I'll chow you one day if you want," said Jean.

"No, thanks," said Jane.

"Why not?"

"I like the way I look."

And with that, Jane relinquished her spot at the mirror, leaving Jean to ponder the choices she had made, and the example she had set for her daughter.

Jean arrived to meet Benjamin at a new restaurant in his neighborhood. The light inside was so bright, Jean felt, as to expose the tricks of self-improvement, and as they took their seats she wished she had heeded Jane's advice and skipped the effort. But before she could excuse herself to go to the bathroom for a check-up, he was smiling at her in a way that made her feel strangely accepted.

It was common for Jean to feel this way—unsettled, unattractive—when she sat face-to-face with a man, unhidden by a phone, not enclosed by an office. With Sam, she felt safe but not seen. They coexisted like compatible ghosts. Uncommon was to feel safe and looked at, neither critiqued nor admired. She felt this way at the moment.

They ate a delicious meal with pleasure, savoring the odd textures—a fish-flavored broth with an orange egg, something spicy with apple, noodles as smooth as the broth they were cooked in. Throughout, Jean waited for the right moment to tell him, privileging Benjamin's news over hers—the trip, a situation at work, a very cool sofa—until she finally dropped or forgot the agenda she had brought to the evening. She began to shed her self-portrait.

"I have some news," she said as they walked toward Ben's apartment.

He stopped, turned to look at her face.

"I'm pregnant."

He seemed to stop again, as though the news had sucked him downward. Then, he nodded and looked to her, at her eyes, looked away and again nodded.

"I'm sorry," she said.

"*I'm* sorry," he said.

"It's no one's fault." She paused. "Or rather, both of ours."

"It was really irresponsible," he said.

"It was," Jean said. "Are you angry?"

"If I am, I'm angry at myself."

Jean nodded. She took another step as though to combat the weight of the news.

"It's a shame we didn't meet ten years ago," he said.

Jean stopped. This struck her as mean, a consolation.

"Yeah," she said. But she didn't mean it. She was glad they had met when they did. She forced herself to take another step and realized they were walking again. They walked at another minute in silence. "So, what do you think?"

Another long moment passed before he spoke. "In some ways, this is the thing I've wanted most. All I've ever wanted. It's a shame. Two nice people. It's tragic we can't keep it."

Another block passed before Jean spoke.

Jean stopped again as anger closed up her throat. "I can," she said.

He turned to face her, and they stood on the the street, canopied by trees, in a typical movie two-shot.

He nodded slowly. "Do you want to come upstairs?"

That night, they stayed up late and talked, trading stories, photos, secrets—Benjamin's laptop propped up on their knees. Kind-eyed gorillas, snow-capped peaks, lions, women in burkas, glittering water of every shade from gray to black to silver. These were the images of Benjamin's life, the evidence, impossible as it once seemed, of a real and vibrant life, an imagination colored by curiosity and the quest for adventure.

"What do you love about traveling?" Jean asked. The computer was their personal projector.

"I grew up in such a small place, with so little perspective, no sense that I could ever get out, that there was any other way to get there. I like to see things. To understand the totality of life."

Listening to his snapshotted stories, each one preserved by its simple frame, Jean felt an all-consuming rush that was like being pulled by a tide. It was both an exhilarating honor to be privileged with the contents of another person's heart, and a fearsome pull to be carried into its current.

"Oh Jean," her mother said when they spoke. "This is terrible news. I'll make the appointment."

"I'm not sure I want to do that," said Jean.

"There's really no choice," said her mother.

"I'm pro-choice," Jean said slowly.

"Jean, you are a married woman. And a mother of two. You have no choice. Now, get in the shower, put on some clothes, and I'll pick you up at noon."

Jean's response was to hang up the phone. A week had passed since they spoke.

Now, as Jean sat in her doctor's office, her legs a shade lighter than her pink gown, she wondered if she had been too quick to dismiss her mother's advice. But none of this seemed relevant as she gazed at the black-and-white blur on the screen, as the doctor offered a pair of headphones so she could hear the fetal heartbeat.

"You sure you want to do this?" asked the doctor, holding up the headphones as if the sound of her baby's heartbeat alone would make up her mind.

Jean looked at the doctor and back to the screen, its rounded image still unformed despite its frame, her own body. She thought for a moment of the man sitting in the waiting room outside. She nodded, extended her hand, and put on the headphones.

"Can you hear it?" asked the doctor.

Jean said nothing, shifted in her seat.

"That's the beautiful fetal heartbeat. Do you hear it?"

Jean nodded and smiled, stared at the clarifying blur. She had become the movie on the screen. She had produced this image.

Benjamin was not in the waiting room when Jean came out. He was standing outside, facing the street, like a wolf trained on the moon. Jean tapped him on his shoulder before he noticed her.

"Want to walk?" he asked.

"Sure," she said. They turned into a park and walked through the trees in silence.

"How do you feel?" he asked.

"Okay," said Jean.

"Good. I'm glad."

"You?"

He frowned and turned away.

"It's going to be okay," said Jean. "Whatever we decide."

He turned back to face her. "Decide?"

Jean stopped and stared at Ben.

"I must have misunderstood. When you said I should come—"

"That was a checkup," Jean explained, "to figure out how far along it is, and, if we choose to terminate, to determine the right procedure."

"Oh my God," he said.

Jean nodded, shrugged, shook her head.

"Oh my God," he said again. His lips were wet, mouth parted.

"I can't tell whether you're relieved or disappointed."

Benjamin shook his head, scanned Jean's eyes. "Me neither," he said. "Which one are you?" He took another step toward her and pulled her into his arms and they stood like this so long that Jean forgot he had asked her a question.

Twenty-seven

The need to tell Sam was all-consuming. Keeping the secret almost felt worse than the secret itself, so old and ironically strong was their friendship. Not to mention the plastic contraption in her bag, its ridiculous proof, like a legal exhibit. But this—her own urine on a plastic stick—was not the most damning evidence. She had committed the crime, maybe the only crime, he could never forgive himself for forgiving. Perhaps he could forgive extramarital sex—couples often do. But how could he forgive such successful sex, sex with this lasting imprint.

Sam might forgive her for stealing, for lying, for breaking something precious, for killing in self-defense. But this was a crime without recourse. Or rather, a recourse without redemption.

Still, even while Jean stomached the nausea of shame, she experienced the equally unsettling sensation of hope. It was unsettling because of its incongruity, like laughing in a graveyard.

That this relationship would also experience gradual decay was a case that was easily made, but mercifully forgettable for now, like when Marty and Jane asked Jean if she would be dead when they were grown-ups.

"Yes, but not for a very long time. Like when you're a hundred," she would say.

The prospect of time's awful and wonderful power was distant enough to push out of her head.

For now, she had plenty of nice things to do, nice things to think about. She must wait and sleep and eat healthy food and take vitamins. This was all she had to do to make a human being. After so much struggle, pregnancy felt immeasurably relaxing.

It was this confusion of feelings that compelled Jean to talk to Sam even before she knew what she was doing. Sam's roles were varied; he was her anchor and her wave, her love and her loathing. The loneliness of their relationship had created a void, a hunger that drove her to this—Jean told herself this, well aware that it might be the most convenient of fictions.

There was no cure for the guilt, even as there was no cap for the anticipation. That she must live with this duality— this would be her punishment. To expect absolution from confession—only the very religious believed in that. And the very guilty.

"Sam, I'm pregnant," she began.

"But we only . . ." He paused. "We rarely . . ." He stopped and scanned Jean's face. "When?"

"Three weeks ago," Jean said.

Sam nodded, tried to picture it, nodded again. "Oh right," he said. "That morning."

Jean looked down at the blanket.

"Well, what do you want to do?"

Jean felt the blow in her chest. This man, this decent, innocent man, was looking after her, was asking for her opinion.

"We certainly aren't prepared for three. Two is almost too much."

"Sam, it's not."

"I think it is. You seem to think so a lot."

"No," said Jean. "The baby."

"What?"

"It's not." She trailed off.

"It's not what?"

"It's not that it's too much."

Sam waited. "What is it, Jean?"

"I did this." Jean paused, repeated. "I did this. With some-one else."

Sam seemed to turn into a different state, like ice turning into water. "Someone else?" he said.

Jean nodded.

"Who?"

"Someone you've never met."

Sam stood, head cocked as though he had heard something in the next room, the same gesture he used to make when he heard a baby crying. His expression changed as his face drained of all emotion. "Oh," he said. That was all he said. Then he stood and left the bedroom.

Sam intended to email Doug, as though he could kill him with an email—a poignant show of faith in the power of language. But before he could write or speak, he threw his computer at the wall, deforming its clean metal cover.

Jean watched from the door as Sam stared at the damage.

He turned to Jean, eyes wet and bloodshot. "How could you do this?"

Jean shook her head, afraid to speak. The answer was worse than the crime.

Sam yanked his phone from its plug and pointed it at Jean like a weapon.

"What are you doing, Sam?" said Jean. "Be angry at me, not him."

"I am angry at you. But now, I'm going to call Doug and his wife. I'm going to tell them their happy little life is over just like ours."

"It wasn't a happy little life," said Jean.

"Mine was," said Sam.

"It was big and sad," said Jean.

"No," said Sam. "Just for you."

Sam paused, as though to consider something new, then seemed to decide against it, then he turned to the phone and dialed the number saved for just this occasion.

"Stop!" Jean said.

She ran toward Sam and reached for the phone. She stood beside him, jumping, pleading.

"Sam, please," Jean begged.

"What," said Sam. "Didn't you tell him?"

The phone was ringing.

"No," Jean said. "Please hang up. Sam, please."

"He doesn't know?"

"No."

Another ring.

"Why not?" said Sam.

A click and a warbled voice could be heard—Doug or Doug's voicemail.

"Please!" Jean yelled.

"Why doesn't he know?"

"Because."

"Because what?"

"Because it's not his. It belongs to a different person."

Here, at least, Sam's face took on the mark of emotion. Disgust wrinkled his upper lip and despair pulled his eyes to the ground. He deprived Jean the solace of another word. He simply turned toward the phone, silenced its warbling speaker, and walked out the door and away from the wreck of their marriage.

Twenty-eight

The complexity of the situation surpassed anything Jean had known. She was pregnant by a man who was not her husband, despite her longtime infatuation with another man (also not her husband), and neither of these men— the two latter, not the former—was the father of her children.

The children. What would this do to the kids? This was really the only question. But Jean had arrived at the answer; or rather, the answer had arrived in Jean's head in the form of hundreds of questions.

Jean knew the stats on this subject, the way divorce could mangle your heart, the way divorce could muddle your future. But didn't sadness muddle more? Wasn't this a risk with pain and heartache? Wasn't this an inevitable result of years of loneliness? Couldn't happiness conquer all, set shining examples of how to love and be loved, how to treat and be treated? Wouldn't happiness take care of everything, make mother and children stronger? Would it be happiness? How could she know? But how could she walk away from the bet given the possibilities, the enormous potential of this particular wager?

And yet, of all the questions that lay ahead for Jean and her children, the hardest thing they faced was this: losing their belief system. Marriage is, in every sense, a kind of religion. Unfortunately, love alone does not sanctify a marriage.

Love, like God and Santa Claus, had a store of evil secrets. It was not kind. It was not good. It was not even very decent. Jean, once a begrudging believer, found herself in an uncomfortable spot of being both doubter and disciple, both savior and sinner. It seemed inevitable that she would break from the religion. The bigger question was what to believe next? How to replace the space that was faith? What becomes of faith when you stop bothering to hope in the first place?

Over the next several days, as Sam's shock turned to rage and rage turned to sadness and sadness turned to something like acceptance, Jean acknowledged a feeling of something like contentment. An amazing sense of calm came with being host to this project.

Contentment was quickly joined by all sorts of opposing feelings: guilt, followed by shame, its more divisive cousin. Somehow, Jean managed—or the pregnancy managed—to produce enough hope to combat the doubts, at least to rival them fiercely, as though hope had its own embryo, imagination.

A doctor visit the following week provided the next reunion.

"Is this a gown visit?" Jean asked the nurse. Benjamin stood next to the table beside her.

"No, not necessary," said the nurse. "You can do this with your clothes on."

"That's what *she* said," said Benjamin.

Jean laughed. "It was *your* idea, genius."

The nurse looked up suddenly, scanned their faces, determined that they were joking.

"Good," Jean said. She turned to the nurse. "We don't know each other that well."

"It's only been a few weeks," Benjamin added.

The nurse looked up again, smiled, then turned back to her computer, no longer certain.

Jean and Benjamin proceeded through the visit in the same satirical spirit, gaining speed as the baby revealed its image.

The nurse stood next to Jean on one side, waving the wand of the machine over Jean's stomach while Benjamin stood on the other side, holding Jean's hand.

A bean-like shape revealed itself on the black-and-white screen, framed by the arch of Jean's abdomen, and outside that, the computer's rectangular outline. As the blur moved on the screen, Ben and Jean watched with wonder, with the combined awe and confusion of being both audience and character.

"Whoa," said Benjamin.

"Wow," said Jean.

He grasped her hand tightly.

And for one moment, it seemed possible that wonder would last forever.

Twenty-nine

A movie crew in preproduction has its own discernible sound, like horses in a barn before a storm. There is a tangible feeling, an electrical buzz, a sense of something imminent. It works on the same principle as a ball on a ramp, propelled by force, mass, and momentum. But a film crew reels from certain invisible factors as well, something that pulls it inward, like a marble around a basin.

"We're gonna move quickly today because we have a lot to cover."

"Famous last words," someone shouted.

"Cover my ass," said another.

Still, the speaker held her own with impressive composure. "I'll never raise my voice," she said. "Not here or on the set, so let me give you one piece of advice. Don't give me cause to."

A cheer rose from the corner of the room with a feminine timbre, signaling that Hair and Makeup was in attendance.

And then, from a different corner, a vying male voice. Lou, the hearty spokesman of the Camera's grip department, announced his presence in the same manner as a policeman flashing his nightstick.

"Okay, so we begin," said Jean. She rapped an imaginary gavel. Jean did an excellent impression of calmness, having learned the best trick of the trade: funnel anxiety with oxygen and push it out as bravado. She sat the head of the large oval table in the waiting area, perched between a blue pleather couch on loan from Noelle's apartment and a desk composed of a plank and two filing cabinets.

Jean had transformed herself since her morning's meetings. She was now the picture of poise, her hair pulled up with a pencil. To her right sat Sam, breathing fast, his fingers playing a drum riff on the schedule handout, a manuscript the size of a Bible. Fanning out next to Sam was his inner circle, lieutenant, and subordinates: Eli, the cinematographer, O'Keefe, the production designer, and Tessa, a wardrobe designer. The four of them looked something like the cool clique in high school had the cool clique openly admitted that they were, in fact, socially awkward. On the other side sat Matt from Locations, assorted members of the Camera department, and a handful of assistants and PAs taking notes for their bosses.

Tessa raised her hand. "Can we start with scene sixty-seven?"

"Let's shoot for scene sixty-six," said O'Keefe, "in about seven hours."

"Shut up, O'Keefe," said Tessa.

"That's what your mama says," said O'Keefe.

"Saddle up, people. Text your wives. This is gonna be a long one."

Just like this—even before the shoot—a crew began to behave like family, a close-knit group that loved each other, shared intimate secrets, and communicated in shorthand— until the last day of the shoot when they tearfully disbanded and moved on to re-create the ecosystem with a new set of people. Still, on a set, no one imagined an end to all this jousting. It was a perfect relationship, one with all the trust of family, all the intensity of a one-night stand—and the same amount of commitment.

To Jean, it sometimes begged the question: what was intimacy really if it could be so quickly conjured and so easily disassembled, then instantly rebuilt on the next production? Was intimacy so promiscuous, a germ that could grow in any hospitable climate? Or was it something more delicate, with more mystery and magic, that only certain people could create, under very special conditions? Or was it both, as common as a weed and as specific as an orchid, its growth subject to time like any other living organism, but, in fact, reproducible anywhere? Like a virus?

It made Jean wonder what other venues could spawn the

same phenomenon. Could it happen in any random subway, a broken elevator, support group, or boardroom? What if soldiers from enemy camps were thrust into the same prison? Could trust sprout between anyone, blossom into something more florid? Conversely, could *anyone* get close to any other person? Could even the closest of friends morph into distant strangers? Given the shifting loyalties of film crews, lovers, and families, it seemed a decent guess to hazard a yes to all of the above questions.

It made Jean feel, over the years, that love was a simple equation, a recipe that could produce a decent result with the right ingredients and timing. Spend enough time together in enough cramped spaces and anyone could fall in love, find a family, form friendships. There was no special alchemy. It could happen in any permutation. And weirder still, Jean had begun to believe in the inverse, that intimacy was finite. It would inevitably combust, just as every film crew disbanded at the end of production.

Sam's cinematographer sat on Sam's left side. Aside from the grips and electrics, the heavy lifters of the crew, he was the heartiest man in attendance. His neck was thick and his face was weathered in the manner of a fisherman.

"Let me introduce you to Josh," said Jean, "our fearless assistant director." Jean spoke very quickly.

Josh, the assistant director, was essentially a human stopwatch. The grace of his job, was to spur efficient work, preferably in silence. A good AD kept things moving at a clip, an essential task when every minute of work incurred the payment of a large crew, the incessant demands of their unions, the rental of expensive equipment, props, locations, and costumes—and, of course, the actors. Time was here, more than anywhere else, a function of money—and vice versa. The ability of a set to stay on schedule was the difference between success and failure.

"Your producer here," Josh began, "is not only smart, but attractive. I caution you: men on the set, just because she is young and pretty does not mean she is not your employer. This director of yours is a talented man and a highly sensitive artist. Bear no mention of the fact that he is"—here, he lowered his voice to a whisper—"a first-timer." His voice reverted to a normal volume. "He is an intuitive and deserving leader and, assuming we do not die of exhaustion, the forty of us are going to make something entertaining and possibly important."

Josh paused as a slow clap began to build volume.

"Thank you," said Jean, silencing the group. "Now, if you'll forgive me, I'm going to move quickly. Please refrain from asking superfluous questions, particularly dumb ones. Some of us have families, others have lives, and the rest would like to get home before midnight. Scene one, we open on a married couple in their private realm. The couple are making love in their bedroom, but they're not connecting. Tensions escalate. Talks blow up. Coitus is interrupted. The camera slowly inches toward our frustrated heroine."

Four hands shot up in every one of the room's quadrants. One from Hair and Makeup. One from Production Design. One from Wardrobe. One from Grip and Electric. Locations seemed miffed to have been left out and added a hand just for good measure.

"Wardrobe," said Jean.

"The nightgown that plays in this scene," said Tessa, "is the same one that rips in scene sixty-seven. I am flagging this for the group because I'm going to need triplicate nightgowns to prevent a major continuity error."

"Would it be so bad," asked O'Keefe, "if the nightgown mysteriously vanished?"

"Shut up, O'Keefe," said Tessa.

"Perhaps the wonders of continuity can be used here to our advantage."

Indeed, the wonders of continuity lay at the heart of a film's magic. Film could make objects appear and disappear, make ghosts of household objects. By accident, the first silent films discovered this supernatural power. Leave a dress on a hanger in one shot; shoot the rest of the scene without it; and poof, as though by the hand of God, the dress has mysteriously vanished.

"Thank you, Tessa. Noted," said Jean. She pointed at Hair and Makeup. "I know that our leading lady has requested extra time in the chair. Theo, I trust you will deliver her to us on time and in good spirits."

"On it," said Theo. "At your service."

Theo's chipper attitude was based on an accurate sense of his importance. Hair and Makeup was the pulse rate of the set. Like everyone else, they were expeditors and hosts, artists whose work was measured in both quality and speed.

"Eli," said Jean, "you are the angel of our schedule. As you know, we're shooting a hundred-page script in under twenty days, which means we have to shoot five pages a day, which breaks down to one page every two hours which allows an average of twenty minutes to light daytime shots, thirty for nighttime exteriors."

"Jean," said Eli. "I've done this before."

"Indeed, we have done this many times together. And that's why I know your talent and your judgment will conspire with our schedule."

Eli was less tolerant of Jean than the others. Jean often found this with the older men on crews. They took her tone to be patronizing when she meant to be direct. "I'll do what I can, but I can't change the time it takes to lay dolly track."

"How much time is that?" Jean asked.

Eli turned to Leslie, the chief adviser in his cabinet. Leslie pursed his lips, shook his head, and made a signal with his hands that meant exactly nothing.

"Can you prelight?" asked Jean.

Leslie exaggerated the same expression.

Eli shrugged. "We'll do our best."

"As you finalize your shot list," Jean said, now addressing

Sam and Eli together, "please note that every dolly takes exactly three times as long as you expect."

"Like I said, we'll do our best."

Jean bowed her head and tipped an imaginary hat.

"One last thing," said Matt, the Locations manager. He was young and very athletic. From his physique, it seemed likely he had scouted every location on a skateboard. "Please note we are still scouting for a location in the greater New York area that doubles as a patch of the Nevada desert. As it is approaching March and we are shooting a scene set on Christmas, I am working closely with Art to get them early access. I'm hoping their plans involve a lot of white spray paint and gauzy cotton."

"Thanks, Matt," said Jean. "I'm aware. Which reminds me, Wardrobe, please tell your younger assistants to go easy on the tank tops."

"My girls are the utmost professionals," snapped Tessa.

"Really?" said O'Keefe. "Last time I saw your assistant, she was using her tongue to apply lipstick to an actor."

"Aren't we shooting nights week one, which means we'd have to shoot night for morning?"

"If you want us to prelight that scene," said Leslie, "you're gonna have to ask nicely."

"Maybe we scrap this location," said Matt, "and go back to plan A, and shoot Jean and Sam's apartment."

Another minor riot began in the back of the office.

"It's Script Day One," Jean announced, swooping in for a

last-minute rescue. "But we're shooting on Shoot Day Ten, which gives us plenty of time to find a new location. Any other questions?" Jean exhaled, surveyed the group, moving counterclockwise, as though daring them to predict another problem. Satisfied that she'd muted the group, she turned to Sam ceremoniously. "Sam, would you like to share any other insights?"

Sam looked up, turned to Jean, his eyes wide and defensive, as though he'd just been caught fanning smoke out the window of his high school bathroom. "Yeah, I..." He paused, cleared his throat.

Jean looked down, prayed for Sam's composure.

"I..." He paused, inhaled deeply.

Jean leaned an inch toward Sam, said a silent prayer. Please don't let this happen. Another painful second passed. And another.

"I'm going to shoot the scene," Sam said finally, "from a variety of perspectives. We'll start with our actress in a tight closeup. Then we'll shift from her point of view to a more omniscient perspective, as though we've craned to see the world from a great distance. We'll shoot out of chronological order to minimize setups. Two singles, tight and over the shoulder. A dolly on her and her p-o-v to establish our heroine's perspective. Then we'll meet the couple in their bed in an overhead two-shot."

When Sam finished, the group was silent, sated and expectant. Sam had passed his first test as a director.

"Got it?" asked Sam.

"Yes," said Eli.

"Yup. Makes sense," said Tessa.

More nods at the back of the room.

"Good," said Sam. He clasped his hands.

"You guys plan that this morning," quipped O'Keefe, "in *your* bedroom?"

"Very funny," said Jean.

"Which reminds me," said O'Keefe, "can you bring in that thing you keep on your desk? The bobblehead thingy with green eyes. We want to use it in scene twenty-six."

"Only if you promise to give it back," said Jean. "The last time you borrowed something for a shoot it ended up going home with an actress."

"Hear, hear!" said O'Keefe.

"I'll drink to that," said Eli. "Going home with an actress."

"You guys are gross," said Tessa.

And the room lapsed back into full-fledged noise, manic chaos reigning again for one beautiful moment.

Thirty

Jean and Noelle boarded the plane, fumbling with bags and conviction. A last-ditch effort to change Tim's mind, though Jean knew it was a long shot. She found the seat and settled into her place, arranged her sundry comforts. She dug inside her bag and retrieved her de facto security blanket. She poked at her phone, sent an email to Sam, for the kids, a routine goodbye note: practice the piano, stick up for yourself, learn a second language. And then, as she fumbled to turn it off, an unexpected email from Tim's agent.

"Can you switch to Friday at six?" it said.

Jean stared at the screen. Those who are always braced for disaster tend to react the fastest.

"Get off the plane," Jean declared. She lunged from her seat, yanked her bags to the floor, smacked at the overhead compartment, then forged her way up the aisle, fighting oncoming passengers.

"What are you doing?" Noelle said.

"Come on," said Jean. "We're getting off the plane right now. He's postponing the meeting." She marched with force up the aisle, Noelle trailing behind, gradually making her way to the front of the aircraft.

"Excuse me, we have to get off this flight," Jean informed a flight attendant.

"I'm sorry," he said. "We're clocked for takeoff."

"It's imperative," said Jean. "I'm canceling my trip. There's been a change in my schedule."

The attendant looked from Jean to Noelle, gauged the ferocity of Jean's intention.

Noelle followed Jean to the door but stopped at the edge, inside the plane, as Jean leaped across the divide into the safety of the jetway.

"Get back on the plane," said Noelle.

"No," said Jean. "I'm sick of being fucked with."

"They're actors," said Noelle. "That's their job. They are paid to fuck with people."

"I'm sorry," said Jean. "I can't do this anymore. These people have no respect for other people."

"Who needs their respect?" said Noelle. "You just need him to be in the movie."

"No," said Jean. "It's not for me. I don't even know what it's for anymore. Something I don't believe in. I'm not going. You go. You take the meeting."

Noelle stared at Jean, scanned her brain for a new mode of persuasion. A flight attendant approached with a menacing look. Last-minute removals from planes were treated as security threats, not just an inconvenience.

"They've already checked your bag," said Noelle. "Who's going to get it?"

Jean paused, pictured the luggage below, mentally scrolled through her belongings: a silk shirtdress, pair of heels, a sweater, a pair of running sneakers, all expendable when compared to her family, her freedom, her independence.

"I'm not going," said Jean.

Noelle exhaled, stared down her partner. "Don't give up now."

"I'm not giving up. I'm regaining."

"You're giving up in the homestretch," said Noelle. "This is what you do. You do this."

Jean stared at Noelle, mouth parted, no blinking. Noelle had taken aim at Jean's heel and struck the tendon.

The flight attendant approached them now, stood beside them, foot tapping.

Jean closed her eyes. She fought the assault of doom on her heart, as though it were a flame she was eating.

"Let's go down with the ship," said Noelle. "At least we'll know we died trying."

Jean blinked and inhaled. This time, it activated her gag reflex, the full force of her volition. Then facing it down or spiting Noelle—both seemed equally possible at this moment—she gasped for a last breath of earth's fresh air and marched back onto the airplane.

"I promise good things will happen," Noelle said as they fastened their seat belts.

But Jean did not care anymore. She had passed from the land of good things to the realm where nothing really matters.

Thirty-one

Jean and Ben met later that week when Jean returned from her mission, determined to decide, in a bar on a weekday, the course of the future. This time, they sat in somber silence while they stared at their orders, but remained somehow unified in doubt—a difficult feat—silent but connected.

Ben looked at her now suddenly, as though he needed to share a secret.

"Talk to me as though you were talking to someone else," she said.

"Okay," he said, breathing out. He seemed relieved by this assignment. "So I've been dating this girl."

Jean nodded, felt and faced the full weight of his disclosure.

"And then there's this other girl with whom I've been having a friendship. This girl, this friend, is, hands down, the smartest, most interesting woman. In fact, I once broke up with the other girl because, in comparison to this girl, the other one seemed, you know, boring."

Jean smiled, overwhelmed by the revelation. Her challenge here—she had worked for this honesty—was to remain silent.

"So this friend, we see each other a lot. We go out to dinner. We go on bike rides. We do things. We're having this wonderful friendship, these magical experiences. And when I'm with her, I feel totally comfortable. But it turns out, we're not friends at all. We're having a serious relationship. And we could have a serious future."

Jean paused, smiled, nodded. The collision of logic with hope was one of life's most intense feelings.

"So it turns out this girl, this friend with whom I've had this serious drunken mishap, it turns out she's the girlfriend, not the friend, that *she's* the one I should be with."

On instinct, Jean turned away, in an effort to hide her surprise. Her face and hands had gone hot. She could not let him see this.

"So the question is," he went on, "what to do with the relationship."

"The friendship?" Jean said.

"The relationship," he repeated. "Do you think there could be a future?" he asked. His voice was high, almost pleading.

Jean looked up, heart pounding. She knew her answer was crucial. "Do *you* think there could be a future?" she asked.

He paused for a moment but not for long, due to fear, not indecision. "I do," he said.

Jean smiled, looked down.

"Do you?"

Jean took in a well of air. What was the right answer? The one that would reap her great desire, the one that would shore up uncertainty, be the future? "I do," she said.

And she allowed herself to float away on the sheer shock of the moment, even as she knew these words, this pure and perfect moment in a Brooklyn bar on a random Tuesday, would vanish as soon as Wednesday's sun rose, as time clicked on in the endless slide show of human emotions.

Thirty-two

Occasionally, Jean attempted to make an honest analysis of her situation. Unfortunately, this required making an honest analysis of herself. The complexities of her marriage, the complexities of Sam, and the complex nature of human relationships combined to complicate the issue into an honest-to-goodness mess.

On balance, Sam was a wonderful guy, a catch by any standard: smart, kind, handsome, devoted to his kids. The first few years of marriage had been comfortable, cozy, and quiet, with frequent trips to the farmers' market, dinners out with friends, wonderfully boring nights at home, big plans for the future. Sam was creative, talented even, arguably a genius at what he loved: telling stories with pictures and words, making things with his imagination.

This had been enough for Jean. More than enough. Perfect. But what had been Sam's shortcoming? What had held him—held them—back? Surely there was something specific? If not, that would mean that the slope of any life, the curve of a marriage, the trajectory of two people could inexplicably come up flat. That effort could not always fix a life. That happiness might be more elusive than that, like luck. That love and happiness might be different.

Much better to ascribe the problems of a relationship to one person, or to people in general, to things like goals and hobbies. Better that than to face this bleaker version.

For years, Sam and Jean had indeed been complementary. Sam was quiet to Jean's loud, thoughtful to Jean's impulsive; he liked obscure foreign films while she preferred comedies. They were opposite directions on the same compass, one flip away on the same coin, compelling evidence of the comforting idea that people behave like magnets.

But the things that linked two people were far more mysterious. Among those things: attraction, of course, with its idiot's eye, its blind devotion to soft circles, its wizard-like power to turn women into cliffs, men into lemmings. But beyond attraction, something weirder wielded power. Novelty? Circumstance? Boredom? Rebellion? The all-consuming and unfathomable urge to break the thing you've built, to hurl a wrecking ball through your life like a child tearing down a tower of blocks?

This had pulled her away from Sam. It was not a repulsion to Sam, but a separate and massive force. Jean wanted to bust from her box, the home she had chosen, built, and feathered, to understand how something could be both a source of pain and comfort. She loathed the very world she loved, the world she had created, loathed it in spite of—because of?—the fact that she loved it so much. And most of all, she loathed herself for failing to love it.

She wanted to break the thing she had made and its precious contents. She wanted to see what it looked like when it was splintered. Did it work as a lens, as a magnifying glass, as a prism? Of course, Benjamin himself presented all sorts of delights. So handsome, so funny, so much fun to be in his presence. The clarity of his eyes, the shape of his lips, the unmistakable sadness, the way it flashed like a road sign in the rain as a plea and a promise. He understood and, even more, he needed her understanding.

But hadn't Sam once flashed the same badge, issued the same request and warning? What happened since she made her pledge to him, chose him as her protected and protector, promised to look after him and to be looked after? Did these promises expire? Could they be bolstered, renewed, restructured? Was it novelty that compelled the need, disloyalty that justified the replacement? Or had Jean chosen wrong the first time, changed fundamentally as a person?

She and Sam had grown apart—this was undeniable. But did this mean people could grow together, merge like a vine and a ficus, one strangling the other until that one takes over? That Jean and Sam could grow apart implied that they could grow back together. If not, then time alone would take that blame, not only to heal all wounds, but also to inflict countless others.

Benjamin existed as a function of Sam, had all but been created from him, like Eve from Adam, a man formed in the image—the opposition, the completion—of another. Ben was bold where Sam was shy, Ben explored the world while Sam stayed home and drew it in pictures. Benjamin "completed" Sam—not Jean. He filled in Sam's shortcomings and, of course, he added his own assortment. His advantage was simply that these weaknesses were not yet known.

Regardless, the sum of all these thoughts amounted to zero. Redemption was impossible and introspection was easy. Not thinking was perhaps the more admirable aspiration.

A few nights later, Sam joined Jean in her hallway office. She stared at her computer as though she had mistaken it for a window.

"What are you doing, Jean?" said Sam.

"I don't know," said Jean.

"What are you doing, Jean?" he repeated.

"I don't know. I haven't decided."

"Jeanie, what are you doing?"

"I don't know, Sam. I honestly don't."

"How can you not know at this point. Don't you have to decide soon? Isn't there some sort of deadline?"

"I have a little more time," Jean said. "In New York state, you have until twenty weeks."

"Jeanie, what are you doing?" said Sam.

This time, she shook her head, as though she had heard him for the first time.

Sam took a step down the hall, approached the children's room, his temporary bedroom. Then he stopped and looked back at Jean, eyes wet, broken, but hopeful. "Ditch him and raise it with me," he said. "I'm serious. Onetime offer."

Jean's heart broke. What kind of man would say this? How could she not love him? How could she love any other? Why was she willing to trade love like this for newness, love of incredible heft and weight for that of a stranger?

Jean smiled and looked away. She had no answers for any of these questions.

It had not always been this way. There had been love and happiness. Both, at once, and together. There had been good times, wonderful nights, laughter, magic, sweetness. But children and romance, any parent knows, are not the best bedmates. Sam and Jean had been prolific, producing two children, a home, many stories between them. But they weren't meant to be. Opposites attract—then slowly drive each other to madness. When they finally acknowledged it was over, they did so with great sorrow, both of them harboring the secret fear that the best—and the worst—times were behind them.

The end of a relationship is one of life's great trials. There's a reason divorce is lumped in with death. Both require the astonishing work of reconciling truth and fiction, facts with expectations. Divorce begins, just like marriage, with simple mathematics: one plus one is now two, divided. Then it gets more complex: there's the calculus of revision, subtraction, the long division of time by expectation, the losses to your heart and home life.

Ten years ago, who would have known—though perhaps anyone could have told them—that Jean and Sam would not make it, that their happiness would be short-lived, short-lived by definition, something beautiful to enjoy that only the foolish covet.

"Most relationships fail," Sam once said.

"I know," said Jean. "It's a scary statistic."

"Ours won't," he said.

"Why not?" said Jean.

"Because," said Sam. "We're building something bigger."

For years, they had tried as hard as they could, as hard as humanly possible. But in the end, they lost their way, or their will, or their good intentions.

Thirty-three

A movie set is a wonderful thing on the first day of production. Each part of the crew rises and falls with its own function. First, the PAs take their surly stations, arriving at the earliest hour, followed by the food trucks, ADs awaiting their charges. Light trucks roll in, then the camera, the Teamsters, the gaffers, the grips. Then actors arrive in their dark sedans, windows up, still napping. Somewhere nearby, the director paces, or buries his face in his drawings. The cinematographer waits in the wings, ready to take instructions. Wardrobe rolls in and assembles their racks. Makeup props up their mirrors. In the span of ten minutes, a crew is born. A crowd of fifty converges and begins to move as one creature.

The producer can take credit for this daily delivery. For Jean, the feeling never got old. The first day on set was like a birthday—so intense was the sustained energy required to bring this all to fruition.

Somehow, the energy was greatest when things went awry—which they did as a rule, particularly when a movie's investors pulled out a month before shooting, a reasonable enough response to the sudden and whimsical decision of your lead actor to take another project because he "just wasn't feeling it," at which point the producer of the now truly independent film—independent of money, lights, camera, and actors—must reconceive the script, budget, schedule, and cast in the throes of the producer's second trimester, while her belly and body began to expand like a Halloween mask, which Jean did with considerable poise despite the simultaneous end of her marriage and beginning of a new relationship with a man who was arguably more of a stranger than the baby growing inside her.

Her solution was simply to carry on with tenacity and purpose, as had been her longtime approach in life and business, and to reconceive the movie with slightly more modest ambitions. And so, Jean and Sam banded together for this very effort, slashing the screenplay by twenty pages, shrinking the schedule from five to three weeks, begging the crew to work for peanuts, confining the grip and electric crew to four, not eight, very tired people, setting the pace of work at such a speed that the actors had nearly to run to find their marks before the call of "action," shooting on digital instead of film, using lamps instead of klieg lights, restricting craft service to cases of Coke and, for snacks, peanut butter and

Ritz crackers, leveraging credit cards to such a hilt as to actually strain the plastic and, of course, buying into the belief so completely as to project confidence where there was stress, delight where there was panic, gratitude where there was concession. It was not unlike the skills required to make a good marriage.

Just like this, Jean and Sam pulled off the most difficult feat of magic: belief in each other and a common goal even after giving up on their marriage. Together, they instilled conviction in their crew and in each other, all good skills to have if you want to lead a movement—or be independent.

Jane was perhaps the luckiest beneficiary of the project as she finally got the gift she had been hoping for at Christmas. With a simple click of the camera, Jane came into her light. Another click. And she rushed out of frame. The locked-off camera bearing witness to the Jane-less image. Jane walked back and forth, in and out of frame, while the camera recorded her movement.

In the editing room, a month from now, Jane would get her wish, would feel firsthand the power possessed only by superheroes and pagan idols. By cutting the image of Jane together with the image without her, Sam gave Jane, on-screen, the gift of invisibility. Jane would appear to disappear, could appear and disappear ad infinitum and, with the simple click of her wand, Jane would have this power forever.

Jane.
No Jane.
Jane.
No Jane.
Jane.
Born and gone. Born again. Just like magic.

FICTION
NIE

Niederhoffer, Galt.

Love and happiness.